"Quality, Protein-Rich Meat Products"
and other stories
by H.M. Friendly

October 6th, 2017

For Michael, to a fellow science fiction fan ☺

Thanks for supporting my dream!

Text Copyright © H.M. Friendly, 2006-2016
Cover Art © night_stomach, 2017
(https://www.instagram.com/night_stomach/)
All rights reserved.
First publication: 25 June 2017
ISBN-10: 1548356700
CS ISBN-13: 978-1548356705
BISAC: Fiction / Short Stories

This book is dedicated to the following people:

– Ann Beck (my editor and mentor, without whose relentless hounding I would not have gotten back into writing after my first and only story I wrote a decade ago ["Close your eyes.", p.103])

– night_stomach (my illustrator, because awesome cover art is to a book as integument is to viscera)

– Andy from Cavity Curiosities (keeps me stocked with mint sci-fi short story collections from last century, and gave me the idea to do this book)

– Alex Gilchrist, Sophie Papp, Al Lindskoog, Amber Overall (friends who graciously endure me pushing my story drafts upon them)

– Moe & Leslie Maynard (my family, who patiently listen to me ramble on for 30 minutes at a time about new plot ideas)

– Ivy & Alaya (my girls, who keep me above water in stormy weather. ♥)

Author's Foreword:

Some decades ago, I emerged as the product of cellular meiosis, and it took me several years to really comprehend the gravity of the fact that I had had the terrible misfortune to be born as a member of the human race. It is perfectly likely that there are billions of sentient, intelligent species in the quintillions of cubed light years in the known universe, and I found myself saddled with one which is obliged to devote entire scientific disciplines to the study of human psychological and sociological pathologies, because there doesn't exist a human among us who is not plagued by at least one of them. However embittered, I am nevertheless relatively stoic about this tragedy, and I work through it by writing stories about fictional people with exceptional quantities of these qualities. I hope reading them distracts you from your human deficits, as much as writing them has allowed me to ignore my own impressive collection of shortcomings. Enjoy!

Sincerely,

~H.M. Friendly

(P.S. If you send me *detailed, productive feedback** on what you like, or hate, about the stories, I will either give you 50% off the purchase of my next collection, *"The New Genesis Series"*, or a 50% refund of the purchase price. Send email to *H.M.Friendly@gmail.com*)

*More than merely "They're awesome!" or "They suck!" Give specific, in-depth examples. Discount/refund is based on the list price before taxes/shipping. Proof of purchase is required. Offer expires December 31st, 2018.

H.M. Friendly is a writer from Victoria, B.C., Canada, who spends his days studying neuropsychology and related sciences at the University of Victoria, and his nights offsetting an absurdly omnipresent sensation of disillusionment through exploration of literature.

Contents

Harvester (sci-fi/horror) 1

"Quality Protein-Rich Meat Products" (sci-fi/horror) 15

Earthship : Devolution (sci-fi) 35

Dragon Catcher (sci-fi/horror) 57

Shrink Your Dead! (scifi/horror) 69

One Thread Short (sci-fi) 83

Close your eyes. (horror) 103

Harvester

The mucous membranes in my nose burn in agony as I inhale sharply, and I taste the familiar sour trickle down the back of my throat. I sit up in the chair, repeatedly sniffling and wiping my nose with the back of my hand. It feels like rubber, and now the back of my throat feels numb, too, but it's fucking great, and I feel the rush as the chemical courses through my bloodstream and my neurons are blasted with an overabundance of dopamine.

I chop out another line from the eight-ball of cocaine, then twist the rest back up in the bag for later. I get up and begin pacing around my apartment, feeling like I can run a marathon, but I know I must wait for tonight's assignment. It will arrive precisely at midnight, just like it does every night.

My apartment is a squalid shithole bachelor on the wrong side of the tracks – the building I live in is ninety-three years old, and if I could guess, it hasn't been maintained in that entire time. My floors are rough, warped boards that bristle with slivers. In the middle of the room is a round throw rug which used to be all the colours of the rainbow, but now it's just brown, green and black. The walls are pasted with a floral print paper, covered in brown splotches and thick with years of nicotine build-up. I can't even scrape it off with my fingernail. The ceiling is yellowed and sagging, from when a pipe must have burst upstairs, and the entire southeast corner is festering with black mould. From the center of the room hangs a single forty watt incandescent bulb on a bare wire, giving the place a murky, clandestine appearance.

In one corner of the place is an old mattress, bare, sagging, and unbelievably stained. I sleep there. I don't have a pillow or blankets. The bathroom is a holy horror, and most of the drywall is missing, revealing the studs beneath, which is home to rats, spiders, and other creatures. I won't even mention the toilet.

I could go on describing it, but I think you get the picture. I sit down again on the wilting La-Z-Boy, and crack my knuckles. I check the clock. *11:56 pm.* I pull the baggie out of my pocket, inspect it, and shove it back in. I get up and pace the floor again. *11:57.* I go take a piss and wonder about a red, open sore on my penis that I don't remember seeing there before. *11:59.* I look at myself in the two remaining shards of mirror above the sink (which only produces brown, murky water imbued with chunks of rust) and I look just awful, and about twenty years older than my thirty-eight seasons. I pull the biggest shard out and throw it at the far wall, where it explodes into myriad sparkling slivers of glass. My watch beeps. *12:00.*

Palms sweaty, I walk out into the living area and stare at the glowing white light beneath my door. After several seconds of this, my vision develops those weird halos you get when you saturate your visual system with too much of one scene with no updated input. Just now, I hear footsteps beyond the door, and a shadow partially extinguishes the strip of light. A small, white piece of paper is thrust underneath, and the shadow quickly draws its footsteps away, down the hallway.

I scramble to the paper and clutch at it with a shaking hand. I hastily unfold it, and read what is written upon it. Then, I produce a book of matches and burn the paper, grinding the ashes into what is becoming a very large black spot on the floorboards in front of the door. I wipe my palms on my jeans, take a deep breath, and exit the apartment.

...

An hour later, I'm walking through the affluent part of town, my dark hoodie pulled up to hide my face from onlookers, and I melt into the shadows. I pull a butterfly knife from my pocket, nervously flipping it open and closed. After a few minutes of waiting, I see two suitable targets approaching – a university-aged couple wearing clothes that probably cost more than my rent.

As they enter the shadow of a tall oak tree, I step out into their path, brandishing the knife in a great flourish. I tell them to keep their fucking mouths shut, or I'll cut out their tongues. They automatically raise their hands and cower, and I demand they fall to their knees. The girl, a wholesome-looking blonde of about twenty, is making wretched whimpering noises deep in her throat, through her tightly clenched teeth.

I order them to give me their wallets and their jewellery, then I command them to strip down to their underwear and give me their clothes. They comply in abject terror, and I turn and disappear into the shadows. A few minutes later, I'm in the bathroom of a 7-11, the loot safely stuffed in my backpack, and I'm chopping out another couple of lines on a tiny handheld mirror with a razor blade. The light is a thick yellow, the sort that makes it difficult to find a vein for the heroin users who like to shoot up. I don't have that problem, and I rail the lines, lick the mirror, and rinse and dry it thoroughly before putting it away.

Then I go home. Tomorrow is another night.

...

I wake up crying again, like I do most nights, because I'm dreaming of my kids. My daughter's name is Cadence, and she's four. My son is named Jacob, and he's six. I dreamed we were eating ice cream by the ocean, and we're having a fantastic time, laughing and tasting each other's cones and such, when I hear my name from behind me, like the whisper of the wind. I am certain it is my wife's voice, so I turn around, but there is nobody there. Then I become aware the laughter and happy voices have plummeted into a dark cavern of emptiness – silence. I turn back around, and Cadence and Jake are nowhere to be found. They're *gone*. They've been *taken*. It's every parent's worst nightmare...

Twenty milligrams of Valium go down easy, and I know I'll fall into the sleep of the dead. Truly, in a few minutes, I no longer worry about the safety of my children, or anything else.

...

I used to have it all. *The American Dream.* My wife, Kate, was a hot-as-fuck strawberry blonde with a great rack, a fantastic ass, and legs to her shoulders. I had a decent job as a pharmacist at a little dispensary in town. I'd come home every day to a nice house in the suburbs, and the first thing I'd hear was the drumming of little feet as the kids galloped down the hallway and nearly tumbled down the stairs to greet me in a flurry of excitement. On my bedroom wall there was a watercolour painting they had given me one Father's day, painted with a chaos of blue and yellow as the background, upon which was scrawled "♥ dAdY" in red fucking letters. Now I have **nothing**, because ***they*** have it all.

Who are *they*, you might ask?
...
Ten years ago, nobody had ever heard of *Vicarious Living Solutions*. Now, it's what people save up their vacation pay for. Nobody cares about Caribbean cruises anymore, because everyone has done that. VLS recognized that people want to do things they've never done before, and what's more, they want to do things they'll never get to do, ever. People in wheelchairs want to play football and perform ballet, old women and men want to be young again, poor people want to be rich, the chronically sick want to be well, the lonely want fulfillment.

VSL created the *capsules.* For a hefty fee, they'll bring you in and interview you to find out just what *Vicarious Living Experience*®™ is right for you. They'll give you a full physical, administer a psych and personality assessment, assay your family and personal history via a thorough cross-examination. They'll attach electrodes to your skull, and several different nutrient/hydration IVs in your arms. You'll sign a waiver, strip naked, have a urinary catheter and enema tube inserted, then, they'll lead you to a giant capsule shaped like a grain of rice and made of transparent fiberglass, with hinges allowing it to open widthwise. It's filled with a transparent purple jelly which is electroconductive, and they jam a breathing tube down your trachea, and submerge you in this jelly, before shutting the lid.

Then, they administer a sedative to induce a coma-like-state, and you begin your Vicarious Living Experience.

Within your dream-state, you are fed an immersive scenario, but it's not like watching a movie, and it's not like virtual reality. It *IS* reality. Using a combination of pre-harvested experiential data and your own subconscious memories, you enter into a totally immersive world where you *really are there.* You're in control of your own actions, your thoughts, your words.

You're living the dream, and in this dream, you can do whatever you want and *BE* whomever you want, according to your agreed upon consultation. You remain in stasis for as long as you can afford, and when it's done, you retain all those memories, as if they were your own true experiences. You go back to your regular life, and you think, *boy, I remember when I was a rock star, that was awesome. I **can't wait** to do that again!* And you go right back to saving every penny, anticipating that moment when you can afford to return to *Vicarious Living Solutions*. It's a legal, socially acceptable drug.

But there's a technical hurdle to overcome, and the vast majority of *VLS* clients are totally unaware of it. Recall: *"... a combination of **pre-harvested experiential data**, and your own subconscious memories..."*. As brilliant as they are, the VLS scientists can't create a realistic experience out of nothing. Such early attempts yielded nothing more than cheap CGI and *Oculus Rift* three-dimensional VR technology. It was clever, but totally obvious it was a simulation. *"Real Life"* is just too detailed and too variable to be able to create believably from scratch.

So, they employ *Harvesters*, off the record and under the table, to create custom-tailored experiences. I am one such Harvester. I had a neural implant installed which records my sensations and perceptions, and every week, I would receive an assignment.

The assignments are tailored to each Harvester. I, for example, would not receive a "rock star" assignment, because I can't play the guitar or sing. But I might receive a "popular playboy" assignment, and be a rich, good-looking sexy single, with women crawling all over me. That's not too hard to orchestrate. The nature of the assignments vary as much as people themselves.

Kate didn't know about it. I had to sign a non-disclosure agreement stating that the position was confidential between myself and *VLS*. It was a job which paid very well, to supplement my average income as a pharmacist, and it was unique and interesting.

But, slowly, things started drifting South...

First, assignments began coming more frequently. From once a week to twice, then three times, and the assignments kept getting stranger and stranger. One unavoidable aspect of a service that allows people to vicariously experience *anything*, is that there are a lot of people who want to do a lot of fucked-up shit that society won't allow, and it all must be pre-harvested by a person such as myself. Yeah, it's a dirty job, but somebody's gotta do it.

At least, that's how I felt at first. Little things like BDSM encounters, even homosexual encounters, these were not a big deal for me. Once, I researched how to boost cars for a client who wanted to steal a "Batmobile": a 1970 Chevrolet Corvette. I lifted the thing at 12:30 am, rode it around the whole night, then refilled the tank and parked it back where I got it, before dawn. Back then, I would get my assignments during the day, in business hours, so I could fulfill them without Kate noticing. Sometimes, like the Batmobile, I had to make exceptions, but for the most part, I just picked a casual Saturday or something, and no one was the wiser.

Then, they started getting worse. *Much* worse. Muggings, like the one I had to do last night, were just the tip of the iceberg. I was getting assignments calling for me to beat up a particular person that a client might despise, or to kidnap and drown their neighbour's yappy dog – things that I just didn't feel okay with.

So, I stood up for myself.

No, I'm not doing these assignments. I told them. *Above-board, clean stuff only.*

"That's not an option," they told me. "We have client demands to fill. You signed a contract. You *MUST* do these jobs."

It's not even a legal contract, I told them. *I can quit any time I want. Go fuck yourself.*

They told me I had forty-eight hours to reconsider, and I didn't take them seriously. Two days later, I came home to an empty house. The door had been kicked in, the windows broken. Chairs and tables were overturned. Signs of struggle were rampant. I was sick with worry – I tried dialling Kate's cellphone, and to my stupefaction, *Vicarious Living Solutions* answered. They told me they'd call my house phone on a secure line, then hung up. The phone in my hand immediately rang, I answered it, and this is what they told me:

"You were warned not to fuck with us. Now we have your family. We are not above sending you your children's fingers and toes, one at a time, until you fulfill your contract. We have clients who will pay good money for that sort of Vicarious Living Experience, anyway. If you contact the authorities, you will never see your family again. Honour your agreement, and they'll be fine."

I was reeling. I couldn't see, I couldn't breathe, I was sick to my stomach.

But, of course, I immediately capitulated. When I told them I'd do anything, they thanked me politely, and let me talk to Cadence and Jake for a bit. They were crying, and I tried to comfort them, but the phone was taken away. I demanded to talk to Kate. They refused, but I could hear her in the background, terrified, pleading for me to do what they said, and, indeed, I had already abandoned any idea of justice. I just wanted my family back. If it meant I had to spend the next twenty-eight weeks doing dirty jobs, I'd do it.

Hang on, little ones. Daddy's coming. Stay strong, Kate, I'll see you soon.

...

I was fired from my pharmacy job for stealing morphine and benzodiazepines. I had developed severe insomnia – I needed something for it. I couldn't risk calling attention to myself by going to a psychiatrist for a prescription, so I just exploited my position. Got sloppy, though. Was coming into work wasted, and this was noticed. They began keeping an eye on me, and I was too messed up to realize it, so the first time I tried to restock, they caught me and canned me.

"You've been an excellent employee," said my supervisor, an older man with white hair and a kind, concerned face. "I'm very saddened by this situation, and very disappointed... I don't know what is going on in your personal life, but you're a good man, so I'm not going to press charges, but *please*, Jack, get some help! Take care of yourself... and your family!"

Suddenly, I had become a full-time Harvester.

I began doing more drugs, to distract myself from the anxiety and depression which enshrouded me whenever I was unlucky enough to stray a thought upon my family. Biblical wailing and gnashing of teeth; **this** *is hell.*

That was four weeks ago. Since then, my assignments have included kicking the shit out people, vandalism, shoplifting, burglary, and torturing to death a variety of small woodland creatures (seriously) including somebody's four-week-old kitten who shat in a neighbour's award-winning petunias. I was instructed to wedge the poor thing's head under my car tire and slowly accelerate until it popped. You can't believe the screams that little thing made. I vomited all over my stick shift.

Two weeks ago, I had to stab some fat, sexist asshole to death behind some seedy bar. He was a scumbag, so I didn't much mind doing that, but then, last Friday, I was forced to date-rape this young college girl. I charmed her in the bar, got her hammered, then took her home and overpowered her on the bed, despite her drunken protests and rather weak struggling. She wouldn't stop crying afterwards, and I couldn't even wear earplugs, because I was recording. I had to sit and watch her bawling, curled up in the shower, the water flowing from beneath her naked body streaming red.

I'm not a monster though! At first, I had refused to do it, but the next day, they slipped a damp, dark envelope under my door, instead of the usual assignment. It contained my son Jake's pinkie finger. It was fresh, and included a Polaroid of him, holding his hand, bleeding, and screaming. I did twenty-five milligrams of morphine and a mickey of rye whiskey before I could stop sobbing and force myself to go find and abuse this poor girl.

...

One thing that always weighs heavily on my mind is that it's not easy getting away with this stuff. It's not a movie set. This is *real life.* These are *real people* I'm hurting, all to indulge some sick fuck's fantasy world. And *I'm responsible for it all!* I'm accountable for my wife and kids being kidnapped and held in some basement somewhere... and I'm to blame for Jacob's finger! Dear God... I can't think of what they've done to Cadence and Kate, or what they *will* do!!

All I know for sure is, I don't dare cross them again, not if I want to see my family again, alive and with no more pieces missing.

...
It's 11:59 pm again. I'm pacing again. I ran out of blow at 4:07 pm. I haven't eaten in two days. Now, the clock strikes, and the assignment comes. I unfold the paper with hands that are so shaky I drop the thing twice before I get it open. I read it, and immediately, I have to sit down. I look over at the envelope containing Jake's finger, shrivelled, black and crusty, the blood now dried. I stare at it, willing myself to overcome my raging emotions.... but this one, I can't do. I just can't!

Remember 1996 in Boulder, Colorado? Child beauty pageant queen JonBenét Ramsey was six years old. She had bright blue eyes, a charming smile, and shining blonde ringlets. She looked like this:

On the evening of, December 25th, 1996, JonBenét was raped, strangled, and bludgeoned to death in her basement by a family friend, and later discovered by her parents, a pitiful, bloody mess beneath the Christmas tree, surrounded by her newly opened toys, and torn, brightly coloured wrapping paper.

My assignment is to re-enact this incident... I steady myself against the wall and close my eyes, gritting my teeth. I... *I can't fucking do it!!* It's beyond wrong: it's sick, it's *evil!*

I feel nauseated, and I have to lie down for quite a while, but I can't get my daughter's face out of my mind. *If I don't do this...* then... *Oh, Jesus, what are they going to do to my little Cadence?! I can't let her be hurt!!*

With a supreme effort, I get up, burn the paper, and crush it into the floor. I dig through my backpack for the bag of crystal meth I scored earlier today. I'm gonna need some chemical strength for this. I vaporize a massive rock and within only seconds, I'm ready to do anything.

...

The streetlamp casts the building in an eerie glow. I'm hiding in a tree across the road, watching through binoculars. It looks like nobody is around, but there's a car parked out front, so I know somebody is there. I look at my watch. *2:12 am.* I take a deep breath and scuttle across the street, keeping out of the lights. I make my way around the rear of the building and find the back door. It's locked, but I force it open using a crowbar. With a groan of suffering metal, and a crunch, it opens, and I listen for an alarm. Nothing.

I creep inside and move slowly down the hallway. The lights are off; I'm entombed in darkness. I'm not sure where to go, so I quietly open doors and peer inside. But these rooms are empty. I continue on, then round a corner and jump back quickly: there is an open door spilling a triangle of yellow light into the hall.

Whoever's in there, I need to take them my surprise, or I'll never even have the chance to succeed. I *can't* fail at this!

I take a deep breath, creep up to the door, and peek inside. A man is sitting at a table, working on a computer. The clatter of the keyboard covers the sound of my footsteps and gives me courage. I sneak up behind him, my weapon raised. Lunging forward, I swiftly pin him around the throat with the crowbar, and he's gasping, gagging, and choking. I drag him to the floor, crushing his windpipe and suffocating him, until he stops struggling and falls limp.

I pull a length of rope out of my backpack and bind his wrists, then I wait. In a minute or so, he groggily comes to, coughing. He realizes he's tied up, and I've got a shining seven-inch bowie knife raised above his soft head, so he doesn't try anything stupid.

"What do you want?" he asks.

"I want you to show me where you're keeping my family!" I hiss, roughly shoving him back against the wall, pressing the knife against his throat. I try to look as dangerous and psychotic as I can muster, but it doesn't seem to be very convincing, because the guy just looks *bored.*

"Settle down, Jack," he says calmly, and I suddenly wonder how he knows who I am. *VLS* has millions of clients. Despite what I've just demanded, it seems very unlikely that a lone technician pulling a late shift will have any clue about my situation. The inanity of my presumptuousness, and the absurdity of his recognition, gives me a chill down my spine.

"How do you know my name?" I demand.

"I know everything there is to know about you, Jack!"

"Then you know where my family is?"

"Yes."

"Are they here?!"

"Yes."

"Take me to them!!"

"Certainly."

I pull him roughly to his feet and hold him by the collar of his white lab coat with one hand, while brandishing the knife in the other. He quietly walks me through a labyrinth of corridors, down a flight of stairs, more corridors and stairs, until I feel completely disadvantaged. For all I know, he's activated a silent alarm via some subdermal contact chip, and he's leading me into an ambush.

Presently, we arrive at an old, shabby wooden door. It is warped and its grey paint is peeling. The knob is tarnished brass. This is bizarrely contrary to every other door in the place, which is new, shiny, and clean, with stainless steel handles, not knobs.

"Open it," I demand, and when he has obeyed, I shove him inside ahead of me.

The inside of this room doesn't look anything like a science laboratory. It's an old cellar, lit by a bare bulb, with rough cement walls, uncovered studs, cardboard boxes, stacks of *National Geographic* magazines, an old water heater leaking rusty sludge, and a rough-hewn wooden tool bench. It even has windows like a cellar: thin, horizontal slits at eye level. I peer out of one and see overgrown grass and a forest extending off into the distance, illuminated by a full moon. This is peculiar, because we're in a commercial district downtown, and it's overcast tonight.

I look around. I don't see Kate or my children.

"WHERE ARE THEY?!" I scream at the short, thin, bespectacled man, who doesn't even flinch. He just maintains his pleasant little smile, and walks over to a nearby wall, upon which is a switch. He turns and looks at the far wall of the cellar, which is the only one of four which is not lit by the bulb above my head. The light quickly drops off into inky black shadows.

He flips the switch with his shoulder, and another single bulb flickers on. I gasp and cry out in horror. Beneath it are two *things*. The first is an archaic white porcelain claw-footed bathtub. Within it reclines my wife. Her lips are blue. Her eyes are milky white. Her skin is grey. She is submerged up to her shoulders in ruby-red water, much of which has spilled out onto the concrete floor. I run over to her, my heart rattling in my chest. I know she's dead, and I reach into the dark water, find her arms, and pull them out. They are unmarred. I drop them and reach deeper into the blood, my hands blindly finding and caressing her inner thighs. My fingertips crawl into a deep, soft gash, within which I know is Kate's severed right femoral artery.

I pull my arm out, my sleeve soaked to the shoulder in blood, and I collapse with my back against the tub, not bearing to look into her vacant eyes. Now, I look up and I see the other form illuminated on the cracked cement. I had momentarily forgotten about it. From a distance it looks like nothing more than a brown, amorphous lump, but as I approach it, I see that it is an old quilt tossed over *something*.

Terrified, I reach down and gingerly lift off the blanket. Just as I suspected, beneath it are two pathetic little bodies, curled up in each other's arms. I fall to my knees, wailing in agony as I pull the smallest one from her big brother's embrace, and hold her against my trembling body.

Harvester

My dear little Cadence looks ghastly. Her eyes are sunken; her body is little more than bones, yet, there is no decomposition, and the horrifying fact dawns on me that if I had come here yesterday, they would have still been alive. I can see bruises on her face and her throat, and when I look beneath her filthy yellow pajamas (the ones I achingly remember giving her last Christmas), I see more huge bruises on her stomach, chest, arms, and legs. This isn't what killed her, though. My daughter starved to death. I can nearly see her spine through her stomach, and her limbs are stick-thin. I gently place her back down, and pick up my son, Jacob. He looks much the same, except he is missing several teeth, and his nose has been broken. I gasp when I look at his hands. They are whole; there's nothing missing! *Whose finger did they send me, then?!* I can scarcely comprehend the idea that perhaps there is some other poor child being tortured because of me.

    I feel dizzy, and I realize I've been hyperventilating. I literally crawl away from the lifeless bodies which I can barely believe belong to my family, and I sit on the cold cement, my knees drawn up to my chin, shaking violently and drenched in sweat. I feel like I'm going to throw up, so I do, and when I've purged, a wave of cold washes over me, and I suddenly remember the lab technician who led me here.

    I scramble to my feet and look back to where he was standing last, expecting him to be long gone, having run for help, but to my surprise, he's still standing calmly, still displaying that pleasant little half-smile.

    I charge at him with a vicious snarl and tackle him to the floor. I climb astride him and grab him by the front of his shirt, repeatedly smashing him into the concrete.

    "WHAT DID YOU DO TO THEM?!" I hoarsely scream at him, my vision blurry with helpless tears. I collapse onto the ground next to him and weep.

    "***You*** did this to them, Jack," I hear him quietly state.

    "What?!" I wipe the tears from my eyes.

    "Just look at yourself!"

    At first I think he's referring to my personal appearance, which I admit I've really let go over the past few months; instead, I look up to see him holding his arm straight out, pointing a long finger over my shoulder, behind me. I have no idea how he got the ropes off; they're not even lying on the floor anywhere, yet I reluctantly follow the direction he's indicating, not wanting to lay eyes on my dead family again.

    But they're gone. So is the cellar. Now, we're surrounded by eternal blackness. A few feet away, a bright circle of light is cast upon a floor of smooth black marble, yet there is no source to the illumination: above us is only an infinite obsidian universe, the same as every other direction.

    Within the center of the circle of light is a glowing capsule made of a clear, transparent glass and a glimmering, stainless steel skeleton. It is filled with a purple jelly, and submerged within is... *me.*

    Speechless, I approach the capsule, my eyes wide, my jaw hanging open. It's me, alright, naked and rigged with all sorts of tubes, wires, and needles. I

Harvester

turn back to the tech, feeling overwhelmed and very much like a frightened, confused child. What's more, I'm coming down off the methamphetamine. My head feels like it's about to explode, I'm exhausted, nauseated, jittery and anxious, all of which actually seem pretty reasonable in this situation.

"What... what's going on?!" I whimper.

"Those bruises on the boy and girl – they were formed by *your* hand. *You* let them slowly starve, while you sat and watched in silence. The woman – you were directly responsible for her suicide, because of what you did to her children!"

"*My* children! *My* woman! I would **never** hurt them!!"

"Have you ever been here before, Jack?"

"Yeah, of course, when I applied for the job of Harvester!"

"Before that, I mean."

"No!" my voice is shrill, belying my frantic bewilderment.

The technician shook his head gravely. "You came to us a year ago, Jack. You were a lonely middle-aged man, a long-time drug abuser from the projects. You never finished high school. The only jobs you ever had were harsh labour or minimum wage slavery, and even those you couldn't hold for more than a week. You'd inevitably come in loaded and get fired. You collected welfare, and squatted in an abandoned house at the edge of town.

"You've never had a family, Jack. You've never even had a girlfriend. You've had plenty of hookers, though. You paid them with drugs. But you desperately wanted a family. It's the *only* thing you ever wanted, even as a kid, growing up in an abusive home with your co-dependent mother and her multiple boyfriends who drank until they blacked out, then knocked your mom around and raped her. They beat the shit out of you, too, and one of them even fucked you until you were a bleeding, sobbing mess, even more often than he did your mom. With your life a constant reminder of this violent history, you yearned for the "normal life": the cute house in the suburbs, the white picket fence, a wife and kids, backyard barbecues, school plays, piggybacks and horsey rides. But you knew you would never, ever, have a chance at it.

"So you came to us, for a Vicarious Living Experience, but you didn't even make it to the profiling stage. Unprompted, and at great length, you told us your entire life story during the initial, precursory interview, and it was more than we needed to know to determine you couldn't afford us in a thousand lifetimes. But you begged and pleaded, so we agreed to provide you our services, once you had gone through rehab, then fulfilled a contracted period as a Harvester. You see, we had a constant and ever-increasing demand for Harvesters, but we couldn't use you if you were a mess. You agreed, and actually went through with it. You were serious and earnest. When you were three months clean, you got your ticket from us, and began work eagerly. We were surprised, and impressed.

"At first, you took your weekly assignments and all was well. It was the usual stuff: skydiving, jet skiing, cruises in speedboats and luxury vehicles, even some scripted gigs like "secret agent" or "man is irresistible to gorgeous women", stuff like that. This last one was too much for you, though. You couldn't bear the falsity of it, and regressed. Although we didn't know it at the time, you started using again, and to support your habit, you asked us for extra work above and beyond your contract, for which you could be paid on a per-assignment basis. We refused.

"A while later, you came to us completely strung out, with a long proposal on how you could offer us a service you insisted we *couldn't* refuse: entry into a niche market. You would secretly harvest data which would appeal to the millions of people who lust after the deeds that society vehemently disparages, but are bound by laws and life circumstances to merely fantasize about. They would be charged double, or even triple, and would gladly pay it! You demanded a 40% royalty. It was a multibillion-dollar market, you assured us – plenty of money for all of us.

"Disgusted, we again refused, and immediately terminated your contract. We are a legitimate business operation, and we don't deal in clandestine perversions. You stormed out of our offices, and we thought that was the end of it, until our servers started banking feeds from your sensory recording chip, which we hadn't had a chance to remove. You were going ahead with your plan, alone. We watched in horror as you stole, mugged, assaulted, raped, and murdered. You had some bytehead off the street rig the sensory chip to upload to a private server, presumably to sell on the black market, but he neglected to disable the automatic routing to our servers, so we *saw, heard, and felt* **everything**.

"We notified the authorities, but by that time, you had decided to create your own Vicarious Living Experience, taking it by force. You kidnapped two little kids from a park in a nice suburban neighbourhood, and took them back to the condemned house you were squatting in. You pretended they were your own. You made up names for them, imagined a loving wife was there to share your ideal family experiences.

"However, when the children didn't cooperate, you would beat them into unconsciousness, then "send them to bed without dinner", which is what you called locking them in the basement for days at a time without any food, and not enough water. They slowly dehydrated and starved to death while you recorded it all, and, after they finally breathed their last, unsure of what to do with the bodies, you abandoned the house. The police found them two weeks later – and they didn't look quite as nice as you saw them just now. (He flashes me a sardonic smile.) When their mother heard of their murder, she killed herself – it was all over the news, along with your face, but you were nowhere to be found. You had come back to us.

"You stormed in, took me hostage, and threatened to murder me with the giant hunting knife you were pressing against my throat, unless *VLS* finally gave you what you wanted – your ideal family life. We agreed, but, secretly, we had a different plan. We decided prison wouldn't be adequate punishment for a piece of shit like yourself – you might be released one day, and go rampaging all over again. We couldn't let that happen, so we plugged you in, and, without telling you, we erased your memory and stored you in an unregistered capsule, buried deep in the midst of our other 37,000,000 clients.

"Then, we served you your own sick, twisted feeds. The assignments you've been carrying out – they're simply the data you had already recorded. They amalgamated with your subconscious, and indeed produced a family life, after a fashion, complete with violence, paranoia, and persecution. When we wiped your memory, we made a notable personality modification: we profoundly increased your empathy so that the experience of your own actions would be just as horrific for you as it was for everyone else you forced them upon. In fact, it would be even more so, since you are now condemned to commit these disgusting, unspeakable atrocities over and over again; only now, you're saturated with shame, guilt and self-loathing, unbearably tortured by the omnipresent knowledge that you alone are responsible for the grief, agony, and death of all those innocent people. *And it's tearing you apart, minute by minute.*" The technician smiles, a full, unbridled grin of self-satisfaction.

I listen to all this in bewilderment – is he telling the truth, or merely spinning me an elaborate lie to sow doubt and gain control of a dangerous situation? *Is it possible?* Cadence, Jake, Kate... I... I just can't believe it! It *can't* be true!!

"So, if I'm actually in a capsule, and none of this is real, how are *you* here?" I demand of him.

"Oh, I wrote myself in. I'm just a simple software program, designed for narrative exposition, waiting for the inevitable instance when you storm in here on a justice mission and discover your poor "family". It's all been scripted, Jack. Each of your actions and choices has been predicted and influenced. You are merely an unwitting actor in our little screenplay. How do you think you were able to break into a multibillion dollar corporate laboratory with a *crowbar?!*"

"YOU'RE *LYING!!*" I scream impotently at him, brandishing my knife.

"Well, Jack, at this point, the truth is irrelevant. *This* is your reality, here and now, and your time is up."

I jump out of my skin as a whooping alarm fills the building, complete with flashing red lights. I startle again, as the door we came through, having reappeared, resounds with the rapid pounding of a heavy fist.

"Jack Wilhelm!! This is the police!! You have ten seconds to open this door before we break it down!"

"Oh, shit!" I yelp, desperately begging the *VLS* technician. "Please, you've gotta help me, man! I only wanted to get my family back! I don't know about any of that other shit! I only did that stuff because you guys forced me to! I'm *innocent!!* I swear on my life!"

Harvester

The door trembles as something hard and heavy hits it from the other side with a fantastic crash. This continues rhythmically; it won't be long before they're through.

"Don't worry, Jack, that door is reinforced steel," says the tech, as if reading my mind. I peer at it, and indeed, the thin, warped wood has become precisely as he says.

"I can help you." he offers graciously. "I'll hide you in one of these capsules."

I turn around. Extending endlessly into the distance are countless rows upon rows of glowing capsules of glass and steel, filled with purple jelly and strange people. They fade into the blackness, farther than the eye can see. The *VLS* technician grabs my arm and pulls me on a circuitous route through them, until we arrive at what appears to be the one and only empty capsule in the entire collection.

"Quick, get in!" he urges me. I look down; I'm already naked, and I step inside the capsule, shivering as I sink into the cold, gelatinous substance. I close my eyes as I submerge, and my hand brushes against something strange on my other arm. I grope at it – it is an IV tube. After some cursory exploration I discover electrodes stuck to my skull, multiple insertion points in my arms, a urethral catheter in my penis, and an enema tube trailing from my anus. *I don't remember any of this being applied...*

Suddenly, the electroconductive gel begins to tingle. I open my eyes involuntarily and see that the thick substance has become luminescent, purple and sparkling. Now, beginning I'm confused feel to. Are thoughts my jumbled incoherent and. *Is is is is is is is is is strange these sensations.........Kate?! Happening me what to is?!?!?!??!?!?!///////////////*

...

The mucous membranes in my nose burn in agony as I inhale sharply, and I taste the familiar sour trickle down the back of my throat. I sit up in the chair, repeatedly sniffling and wiping my nose with the back of my hand. It feels like rubber, and now the back of my throat feels numb, too, but it's fucking great, and I feel the rush as the chemical courses through my bloodstream and my neurons are blasted with an overabundance of dopamine.

I chop out another line from the eight-ball of cocaine, then twist the rest back up in the bag for later. I get up and begin pacing around my apartment, feeling like I can run a marathon, but I know I must wait for tonight's assignment. It will arrive precisely at midnight, just like it does every night.

[2016-08-22/02:30:10]

"Quality Protein-Rich Meat Products"
(excerpt from the New Genesis series)

It's the meat. I can smell it in the air as soon as I open the door: I can tell that something is very wrong. I figured it might come to this at some point, but I didn't expect it so soon.

It went from good to awful, literally overnight. In only a matter of hours, the whole thing degraded into a putrid, rotting mess. I couldn't do anything about it. I didn't even realize it was happening until too late. And of course, no one takes responsibility. *It's not our problem,* they always say. *Sorry.* Bullshit. What an utter waste. I throw down the phone and look again through the door.

Goddamnit!! I just got that pork rump roast yesterday; I was going to eat it tonight, but I got up this morning and discovered the motor on the refrigerator had blown: everything had been festering in the artificial tropical heat of the bubbles, all night long. This pisses me off, because we only ever get meat on ration once a month. A bit of pork or beef or chicken. Eat within five days, wait another twenty-five days, eating wilted lettuce and maybe a bit of oats or old, stale bread discarded from the affluent New Society bakeries. Perhaps some shrunken, withered apples, or rubbery potatoes riddled with sprouting eyes... but usually just bars of compressed protein paste, and carb crackers.

Meat day of all days! And management won't even vouch to replace the ration! They'll send someone to repair the fridge sometime between Monday and Friday within the hours of 8am and 6pm, and would I be available during that timeframe? How does one even respond to that??

I responded by hurling the phone at the couch (can't afford to break it) and slamming the fridge door. Because you know what? Soon, I'll be out of this dump. I'm moving up in the world. I got a call saying I have been accepted as a lab technician in the *New Genesis Family Farms,* helping to supply meat rations to the citizens of this fine city... hopefully they have working refrigeration systems. Personally, I don't give a flying fuck about this shithole, but if it gets me out of these Old Society ghettos, I'll worship it as if it were literally a sacred cow.

I grab a stale dinner bun out of the bag in the cupboard, and find it dotted all over with green fur. Great. I look around at my pitiful apartment. It is an ancient relic, decomposing and crumbling around me. The floors are rotten hardwood, gone spongy probably before I was even born, and threatening to break through in a few places I take care to avoid. The ceiling fan stopped working long ago. I tread upon a shabby tapestry carpet, stained or worn through in several places. The wallpaper is so crudely painted over I can still see the floral print embossed underneath the paint, if I look closely. The green paisley sofa (which functions as my bed) has foam bursting from the cushions, and an infestation of black mould, with a population rivalling New Genesis, advancing up the back. And, on top of everything, thick layers of dirt coat literally every surface. Who can afford a vacuum cleaner? It would suck precious electricity I'd rather use to heat my water in the morning for a shower and a coffee. Even then, if I use up my allotted kilowatt hours too luxuriously, as I always do: I spend the last week of the month with shockingly cold showers and revoltingly cold coffee. But no more. Fuck this place. *Hard.*

I heave my bag over my shoulder and step out of the apartment, locking the door behind me. Down the outdoor hallway, all the other doors look just like mine: cracked green paint curling from the damp wood of the door, thanks to this constant contrived tropical biosphere.

I curse at a rat with glowing green eyes I see scampering along a wall. A goddamned nuclear war, and rats just *had* to survive, and they're the size of cats now (which are unfortunately extinct, else they might curb the rat problem. Then again, they might be the size of horses.). Fucking terrifying. The walk to the farm is long, about forty-five minutes, through the slums of Old Society District 56Hl. Derelict buildings of glass, brick, and mortar loom above me, their surfaces cracked and crumbling, the windows dark. We haven't had *proper* (read: legal) industry in OS for almost a century. Now, everything is abandoned and left to decay, just like we do, on our feet, in the ground, or decomposing on the Mound, deep in the Pits. I can see gaunt faces peering out at me from the windows: the homeless-by-choice. It's smart, really. If you have no door, the NG-RPEB can't kick it in spouting bullshit about how *you've been found to blah blah blah and this qualifies you for RePurposing as a Subsection_whogivesafuck*, even though **everyone** knows it's a total fabrication. We Old Society filth are the cattle for the New Genesis elite, and when the agents of deception have the power, it is the victims who end up wearing the lie by force.

So, many live off the grid. No telephones, no electricity, no radio, no monthly meat rations, and no homes. They just fucking live and die like cowardly blind mice, trembling for fear of the farmer's wife.

Well, not me. I'm taking charge of my destiny. And speaking of farms, I took the liberty of accessing *GenNet* to research what a farm is and what to expect, and I must say, I'm pretty damn sceptical. Apparently, farms are delightful places where animals are raised lazily together in cow barns, chicken coops, luxuriously muddy pigpens, and wide-open horse pastures. The pictures were lovely, although I know they were from the 20th century, back before the *Extinction Level Event* that made the world what it is today.

Will I have the opportunity to milk cows and pick eggs and feed baby pigs with a bottle? Unlikely. It sounds *too* lovely, as if, with a name like *Family Farms*, maybe I'll be able to finally feel safe, and at home. But I know it's just another face of the *New Genesis RePurposing Enforcement Bureau*, and R. Janus, the sociopath who runs it.

"Quality Protein-Rich Meat Products"

...

  The border between Old Society and New Society is blatantly obvious: it is a checkpoint where we are intrusively searched, and looked down upon like we are the scum of the earth.

  "Stop! State your identity, destination and business." The soldier stiffly blocks my path with a proton rifle.

  "My name is Persephone Anance, OSFem#4583871; Residence OSD56H8; en route to NSD23B, for employment."

  "Employment in a New Society district?" He steps forward, empowered by his crisp grey uniform with its red trim. "How about I employ you to conceive my child, **whore?** I'll pay you with your *life*." He towers over me. I maintain a strict poker face, but inside I'm shitting my pants. I know this kind of thing happens daily. Any OS resident can be "detained for questioning" without reason or rights, indefinitely.

  "Wenkler, step down." booms a steely voice behind the soldier. "Wenkler" leers at me, then, before I can react, he reaches out and grabs my left breast with one hand and reaches between my thighs with the other. I do my best to contain my breath through gritted teeth – *this is just a checkpoint – the real goal is farther ahead.* "See you next time, sweetie." he croons, and turns away.

  Behind him stands a man in a black and red uniform with more shiny bits on it. He stands a full head taller than the soldier. The giant NG-RPEB officer approaches me. I grasp one hand with the other to keep them from shaking. He looks down on me, and, to my absolute surprise, he speaks gently.

  "Relax... we're not all assholes. Stay safe, miss," he says, and he stands aside.

  The wide, clean streets of New Society lay before me.

  My chest feels like it is tearing apart – I realize I've been holding my breath. My heart is racing; I'm sweating; I feel like a tiny boat of emotions in a dark, raging gale of helpless terror. Words are beyond me; I hug my bag to my chest and force myself to walk with calm, wooden legs, through the checkpoint. As soon as I am out of sight, I lean back against a wall, gasping raggedly, feeling the blood pounding in my temples. I've been assaulted before, only there were three of them, and nobody to come to the rescue. It was a long night.

...

  The Farm looks like no farm I had ever seen on *GenNet.* Occupying at least two square kilometers, the facility is a towering cluster of geometrical shapes. I gawk openly as I wander through it, feeling like a little lost kid. The

"Quality Protein-Rich Meat Products"

complex is divided into multiple roads in a grid system. To my left are rows of hundreds of silver cylinders two or three stories high, with sharply funnelling bodies. They look like the vats used in the old brewpubs for brewing and aging beers. Across the road are tall rectangular buildings of brilliant white ceramic and steel. Across yet another road are rows of what appear to be greenhouses with triangular roofs. The facility stretches onwards to the horizon. A group of men in white coats walk by and openly sneer and laugh at my threadbare clothes.

Oh, shit! I almost forgot!! I duck behind a building and, hoping to hell there are no cameras, I quickly strip off my clothing, down to my bra and panties, then pull on a tight skirt, a low-cut suit jacket that makes my breasts look twice as big as they are and threaten to spill out, and some flat-bottomed slip-on shoes. I draw the line at high heels. This female clothing is so goddamn uncomfortable, and I feel like a sexual billboard, as if I dress this way just so I can give men massive erections with which they feel entitled to assault me. I fucking hate it. But this job means *everything* to me! I quickly twist my hair into what I hope looks like a casually professional updo, securing it with bobby pins.

I kick the bag out of sight under some sort of ventilation unit, then, furtively clutching a little canister of aerosol defensive spray, I make my way to the main office, by the helpful directions of the same workers who scorned me a moment ago, and who now insist on leading me there, one of them holding his hand on my lower back, a little too low for comfort. They call me "baby" and "cutie", and assure me they will see me again. I shudder and open the wide glass doors by massive brass handles shaped like wings.

A wide red carpet extends down the center of the elongated lobby, which stretches at least fifty meters. Marble pillars line the walls, supporting balconies extending six floors up. Some sort of green plant exists in pots all over. I think they're called ferns. I didn't even know they still existed. I finger a leaf. It's fake.

I walk up to the wide, oaken desk (probably fake, also) with its glistening, waxed surface. A bored-looking man sits behind it. Upon seeing me he points a long index finger, waving it dismissively.

"Look, lady, you've obviously got the wrong place. Your kind aren't welcome here. Leave immediately."

"*My kind?* I'm here for the job –"

"Right... Look, sex kitten, you "ladies of the night" may "work the streets," but that's not a *real* job. If somebody here called you, kindly deal with your business off the grounds."

"**Excuse me?!**" *Keep calm, Persephone. Think about the fridge at home.* "Look, I am here for the job interview– Assistant Geneticist – with Mr. Tomakin."

"Quality Protein-Rich Meat Products"

"Pfft." He scoffs and attempts to stare me down with a cold, steely gaze. I won't look away. "There is only one person listed as an interviewee, and he will be arriving any moment, so I would appreciate it if you would quit fouling my air. I have summoned security, and they will *escort* you off the grounds, forcibly if necessary." He looks smug, and leans back in his swivel-chair, placing his feet impudently on the desk.

I force my voice to remain level. "I *am* that person. Persephone Anance. Percy."

The receptionist immediately removes his feet from the table, straightens up, and accesses his computer. "*What?!* We thought you were a man – Percival."

I give a little feminine shrug, and look meek. Of course, it's just an act. I knew they would mistake me for a man. Nobody calls me Percy, but it's the only way I could think of to actually get an interview. Obviously, I am not going to tell them that. I just do my best to look innocent and bewildered. He doesn't seem to buy it.

"Listen, *ma'am,* falsifying information on a resume is a federal offence, eligible for immediate RePurposing." He motions with his hand. I look behind me and see two armed guards approaching.

"I didn't falsify anything!!" My voice sounds too shrill for my liking. "HEY! Get your fucking hands off me!" I snarl, forgetting my plan to be ladylike and charming. The security guards are looming over me now, their huge meaty paws on my upper arms.

"She's resisting," states one. The other nods, and I see their hands move towards the stun batons on their belts. *Oh, God... Those things fucking hurt.* I am so scared, I'm almost peeing myself. I hold my breath and try to keep myself from trembling. My anxiety is rising like a pressure cooker; my hand reaches slowly into my pocket for my defensive spray...

Abruptly, the intercom on the desk buzzes loudly. The two guards pause, and look over to the secretary, who presses a button on an earpiece, listens for a moment, then mumbles something, before pressing the button again. He looks up and, with the tiniest wave of his hand, the two guards release their grip on my arms. Apparently some order in my favour has come down from heaven. I seize the moment to regain my composure: I haughtily pull my arms away and look highly indignant.

"If you'll excuse me, I'm late for my scheduled appointment!!" I say testily, smoothing the wrinkles from my jacket. I turn my nose up at them, and stomp towards a door which I hope dearly is the right one. My knees keep trying to collapse under me. My limbs are stiff; I feel like I have two wooden legs.

The large double oaken doors are carved in undulating spirals, with the chiral image of a long, twisting, Oriental-style dragon slithering up their entire three meters; they open just before I get to them. A little man stands before me; he has the figure of a cartoon stick figure and is wearing peculiar spectacles with odd hexagonal lenses. His dark suit is undoubtedly tailor-made, but still fits him like a cigarette tube fits tobacco. His dress shoes are black with pointed toes gilded in shining, golden, swirling oriental patterns. He has a tiny, razor thin moustache sharpened to pencil points on each side.

"Mr. Tomakin?" I extend my hand tentatively. The man looks down at it with obvious disgust, but, after a moment's hesitation and a barely perceptible flash of a grimace, he takes my hand, briefly vibrates it, then returns it to me as if it were diseased, and he must now go boil his arm up to the elbow.

"*Miss* Anance, I presume. How *creative*." He glares disdainfully up his nose at me, and, with a dismissive motion, orders me to a chair in front of his desk. I sit, or rather, perch. It is absurdly tiny, and uncomfortably hard. He sits in his own massive luxury chair boasting a back which easily extends half a meter above his head.

"So... you are interested in the position of Assistant Geneticist. Okay, let's see here. Age twenty-seven... Says here you grew up in NSD, but attended a university in OSD??" His brow furrows as he digests my dissonant half-lie. I could falsify my district of birth – that was just a small hack into the right circuits of *GenNet*, but the educational records are much more complicated, and, frankly, beyond my skill level.

"Yes. My parents were hit with hard times. My father discovered he had Parkinson's – genetic screening wasn't mandatory when he was born – and dutifully RePurposed himself, but the social RP supplement was not enough to afford my entrance into an NS University." Total bullshit, federally offensive.

"And it says you received... an honours Undergrad, and Graduate's degree... with a double major in Biochemistry and Microbiology?!" He looks stupefied. "You can get that in Old Society?!"

I smile coolly and stare straight ahead, unblinking. "If one is diligent enough, yes. You will find the high quality of my work speaks for itself."

Tomakin clears his throat, and regains his composure. "Ahem, well, I regret to inform you that in New Society, we do not honour OS degrees. *Regrettably*, this means that –"

That you'll work me harder than anyone else, and pay me less.

"...you will have to start at a lower pay grade and work your way up, but I have *every confidence* that in no time at all you will reach pay equity."

Yeah, right. I can practically see the glass ceiling and escalator from here. But still, even shit wages here are at least twice as much as what I make now.

"Of course, Mr. Tomakin; I understand. I am *sure* it is merely protocol, *entirely* out of your control." My words are liquid honey.

"Quality Protein-Rich Meat Products"

He shrugs and turns his hands upwards, in a great show of reluctance. "Well, now that we have that settled, Senior Geneticist Jean-Claude will give you a tour."

...

At first, the genetics labs appear pretty unspectacular – the usual collection of microscopes and culture dishes, centrifuges, rotary evaporators, IR and NMR spectroscopes, and the like. "Senior Geneticist Jean-Claude" is in his late forties, with snow-white hair and a neatly trimmed goatee. He shows me through several identical labs, spouting irrelevant bullshit the whole way along. *The Farm is committed to providing the highest quality products, blah blah blah.* I'm bored.

"So, when do I get to see the livestock?" I interrupt him. He goes red in the face and looks at me irritably.

"Ahem. There is no *"livestock"*, Miss Anance: all original-source viviparous and oviviparous animals have been extinct since the Event, or did they not teach you about that in your *community college*? (I bite my tongue.) The meat products are derived from stem-cell cultures grown in a nutritious substrate. *Surely* you have heard of the process of somatic cell nuclear transfer?" His tone is blatantly condescending, as if he has just asked me if I know what a chair is.

"Yes. It is the process used to create embryos which are genetically identical to the parent organism: forced asexual reproduction, if you will, commonly known as cloning. It involves isolating a female gamete from the parent, and from this egg removing the haploid nucleus with half the usual number of chromosomes. This is replaced with a regular diploid nucleus from a parental somatic (body) cell. The cell then initiates mitosis as if it were a regular egg cell which has already united with a male gamete, a sperm, and fertilized. This forms what is called an embryonic stem cell, and growth proceeds as normal, the cell having been "fooled into thinking" it has created a genetically distinct zygote via the usual channels of sexual reproduction and meiosis." *I know what a fucking chair is.* Senior Geneticist Jean-Claude looks somewhat peevishly disappointed.

"Ahem. Indeed. I will show you the embryos."

We enter a much larger room, the size of at least two school gymnasiums wide and three long. Arranged upon workstations extending the length of the room in long rows which seem to converge into infinite, are countless glass beakers about the size of a human head, which contain bright green liquid. (Later, I learn that the scientists call them "pickle jars".) Within these float tiny creatures – animal embryos, hooked up to nutrient tubes which occasionally emit bubbles from the areas where they seem to impale the frail little bodies. From the labelling, I can see each row is segregated into

"Quality Protein-Rich Meat Products"

a single animal type: some are cows, others sheep, pigs, chickens, etc. They look like little aliens in the gelatinous green liquid: amorphous blobs with gigantic heads and dark purple bulges for eyes. I can see through their skin to bones no wider than a needle, and miniscule organs. I see hearts beating asymmetrically through gossamer-thin striated muscle tissue. *Fascinating! Definitely beats my current job at the state-augmented, state-taxed MegaMart.*

All along the rows of stasis vats are computer terminals monitoring heart rate, temperature, emergence and patterning of brain activity, and other displays I'm not familiar with. The flashing lights and scrolling text make me think of the original Star Trek television series from the 20th century I dug up on *GenNet* – if it has lots of little flashing lights, something important must be happening.

"We have hundreds of these rooms. At any given time we are growing hundreds of thousands of cloned animals for consumption by the citizens of New Genesis." JC says, in a bored tone, as we pass into another room, this one containing much more advanced specimens. Now, the foetuses actually look recognizably like the animal they are supposed to represent.

"What are these?" I ask, pointing to several narrow tubes which all converge at the region approximating the heart of the animal. They appear murky and almost black in the green liquid of the vat, but following the tubes out, I can see that each of them is a different colour, with varying opacities.

"IV lines," JC explains, "Obviously, the animal is too small to locate veins in any traditional sense, so the needle is plunged directly into the heart, and even that is only the size of a kernel of short-grained rice. The needles therefore are extremely fine – in the region of micrometers. Only a single molecule of each compound can pass through at a time, but they do so continually." He looks up at me and answers my next question before I ask it. "The compounds are nutrients, steroids, growth hormones, antibacterial agents, and antifungal agents. The latter two are to decrease the chances of unproductive death, which is a total waste of valuable resources, and the former three are to encourage extremely rapid development. A cow, for example, has a natural gestation period of 274 days, that is, 9.13 months – similar to that of a human. This is completely unreasonable in terms of a sustainable aggressive animal agriculture practice. As a result of the compounds we pump into the zygotes via the brine, and the foetuses via IV, we have been able to reduce this period to 73 days, just over ¼ of the original timeframe."

"But these animals look normal. Wouldn't that introduce complications?"

"*Obviously.*" he rolls his eyes.

We enter an elevator and descend further into the bowels of the farmhouse. Upon exiting, I see that each of the vats in this room is big enough to contain an average-sized border collie, had dogs still existed. JC points to the closest one. The calf in this tank looks normal and healthy, in terms of morphology, but it is obviously very dead – a preserved specimen.

"This is a normally developed specimen, most of the way through gestation." We walk down the row, surveying the living creatures. "These are our consumable specimens, at an equivalent stage."

I'm shocked. Several of these animals have multiple body parts, including heads. Some have limbs in the wrong places, and most of them have abnormally large torsos but nearly nonexistent legs.

"After they're "born" we amputate the legs, because otherwise, they tend to break them by thrashing, which leads to infection and death, so we just remove them at birth. The animals survive just fine like that."

I don't have to believe him, because he shows me. Another level down the rooms are jammed floor to ceiling with wire pens, barely larger than the grotesque sausage-like animals lying in swampy puddles of their own excrement. Their bodies are covered in bright red, raw patches. JC tells me it is a combination of the equivalent of bedsores, as well as the caustic effect of the chemicals excreted in their waste products.

*And we **eat** these things?!*

The worst thing about this room, however, is the oppressively loud, disturbing cries. All of the animals are screaming hoarsely. All they can do in their lifelong prison is writhe, their spinal columns twisting with the force of their endless agony. They quiver their tiny little flesh stumps and shriek, lying half-dead in an acrid puddle of piss, diarrhoea, and blood.

It's horrible! It's too much! I'm reeling with a wave of panic which crests over me and crashes like a tsunami. I suddenly gag, and heave, spitting bile onto the lab floor. I wipe the blur from my watering eyes, and literally run back to the elevator. JC follows casually, a shit-eating grin on his face.

...

On the way up I tell him I'm fine, that it was just a shock, that I'm still on board. He merely looks indecipherably at me, and the rest of the ride is spent in silence.

He leads me back to Tomakin, who produces a thick contract and slams it in front of me like a first year biology textbook. Still nauseated, sweating cold, I read through it as best I can, while in my left ear his wheedling voice narrates the "important bits" each page contains, which he conveniently appears able to sum up in about 1/16th of the actual printed words. I'm not a lawyer; I can't comprehend most of this stuff.

But I *need* this goddamned job, so I sign on the dotted line, in red ink.

...

"Quality Protein-Rich Meat Products"

Over the next few weeks I learn the ropes of the position. My job mainly consists of nuclear transplant and initial development monitoring. I feel like God in a way – I create the initial organism, and watch it grow, checking for any significant developmental difficulties early in the process. Sometimes a clone will go afoul immediately. Possibly the transcription factors are messed up in the nuclear transplant process and the genetic instructions aren't carried out properly.

The most common problem occurs in formation of the morula. This is the initial cell division process that forms a multicellular organism from the single celled zygote. The unique feature of this process is that the cells will multiply exponentially, but the little ball will never get bigger, until a certain point is reached. The zygote will multiply from one cell, to two, four, sixteen, and so forth, forming a multicellular ball: the morula. After a short time, it will become hollow in the middle, forming the blastula, and this differentiates into different types of cells: mesoderm, endoderm, and ectoderm, which will become muscle, organs, and skin in the developed animal.

The issue that occurs is when the zygote becomes, in a sense, cancerous. The cells multiply, but in an unregulated fashion, and rather than staying the same size, the ball of cells expands exponentially with the number of cells. This results in a large tumour which will eventually form a severely deformed creature, which usually dies. If I notice this happening, I terminate the process immediately. No sense wasting resources.

It's really cool, watching the tiny cell become living animals! It's magical in the sense that it is mind-blowing, but it is not a miracle, because it is all explained by biology – except for that first cause which set it all in motion. This still perplexes me. In any case, I've been having a great time down in Sublevel 1, with this stuff. Luckily, I don't have to go down into the further Sublevels – the mutant foetuses and tortured animals give me the creeps. At least at the point I am working on, before the immense chemical cocktail has taken effect, the creatures I'm working with are still natural creatures, albeit clones. I'd rather not think of the later stages.

But I *can't* not think of them. Those screams, the wild, desperate, rolling eyes, foaming mouths, lolling tongues, and the smell of vomit and excrement – it haunts my dreams. And, I now forgo the meat ration I so coveted before... Irony, right?

On the walk home, in my ratty OS rags (I don't dare to wear my good clothes past the border: that's just *begging* for a violent rape and mugging in the vile slums I call home) I look up at the giant billboards posted all over town. They show images of a peaceful, idyllic farmland with rolling green pastures, trees, and a beautiful orange and yellow sunrise. Cows, pigs, and chickens idle listlessly in pastures, pens, and coops, without a care in the world. The caption reads: *New Genesis Family Farms: Quality Protein-Rich Meat Products For You and Your Whole Family!* I scoff. Quality, sure, but exactly what quality? The meat products we churn out are the afterimage of

"Quality Protein-Rich Meat Products"

a life of medieval torture and the creation of chemical Frankenstein's monsters. I discovered this old 19th century book on *GenNet* last week. A mad scientist creates a single abomination out of dead flesh. We, however, create millions of abominations out of living flesh...

...

When the animals reach slaughtering age, we don't bother wasting chemicals euthanizing them, we do it the old-fashioned way, tried and true, perfected back in the early 21st century:

A worker grabs an animal by the head with an electrified clamp, which stuns them. Then, they are impaled by meat hooks and strung up, and their throats are slit, but lots of times they wake up too soon, so when they're strung up and bleeding out, they're still conscious, spraying blood everywhere, twisting and screaming and choking, and bubbling and frothing like they've just eaten a bar of soap: very, very red soap. Or, the bleedout operation might be botched, leaving the animal fully sensate and alive when it's dropped into a tank of boiling water, which makes the skinning process much easier – just like potatoes.

Sick or dying animals are kicked and beaten and electrocuted by the workers, for sport, then impaled through the brain with a thick, pressurized, pneumatic bolt. Baby animals close to death are savagely brought the rest of the way: they have their heads smashed repeatedly onto the concrete floor until they're just a pulpy mess, or they're stuffed into a decapitation machine, but if it's done carelessly, they might just end up partially decapitated, with only their snout and half their face sheared cleanly off. When that happens, you can see their one remaining eye gyrating wildly, and their pink jelly brains are visible through the gaping hole in the front of their skulls.

Other stuff happens too. It's really horrendous. As an "Assistant Geneticist", I don't have to do it myself, I just wear a white lab coat and supervise impoverished Old Society citizens paid below-subsistence wages with no benefits and long hours. And because I've been there, *I get it:* I fully understand why they unleash their indignant rage upon these helpless creatures. I see the bitterness and spite in their eyes as I perform my "administrative tasks" and boss them around – I feel like a hypocrite. I think, *"Guys, I'm actually just like you, just smarter, cleverer, and a better liar; tough break, sorry about that."*

I admit, it *does* get to me. But everyone in lab *agrees:* they're only dumb animals! The truth is, I have my own life to think of! I really **need** this job! Besides, it's not forever... just until I get settled into my new apartment. Then I'll find something different.

I promise.

...

"Have you prepared the substrate for batches #BVS_64B, #4500 - #4700?" My lab partner, Assistant Geneticist Mason, asks me. He is a little younger than I am, with messy brown hair, a perpetual couple days beard stubble, and walks with a loping slouch. He looks like Shaggy, a character from a 20th century cartoon about a mystery-solving quartet with a Great Dane.

"Bovine Serum 64B... uh... yes. They're ready to go." We are preparing for another nuclear transplant operation. Mason and I have been working together every day since I started here, thirteen months ago. He showed me the ropes and after a while we became sort-of-friends outside of work. We go back to his place and play video games. I don't have anything like that at my place, but his New Society apartment is awesome! There is a holographic media room that places you directly in the middle of a game, as if you are really there. Special eyewear allows you to see normally, but also overlays personalized aspects of your user experience upon your own body, such as outfits, gear, gadgets, and weapons. Motion capture sensors track your movements and put you directly in the action.

I have a home entertainment station, too. It is a kitchen chair with metal legs and covered with paisley vinyl coloured avocado green and amber-alert orange, with yellow foam everting out of several rips and gouges. Beside it is a bookshelf which is missing a shelf, and upon it are a couple dozen books from the 19th-21st centuries, from back when they still made books with paper (before Apple gained an imposing position in government and passed a bill outlawing paper because of "environmental concerns"). I've read all the books so many times I can nearly recite them. Mason's place is way cooler, and, soon, I'll be able to afford a place like that, and an immersion chamber, too!

"Um, I need more Formalin; I have to go down to SubLevel 3." murmurs Mason, his nose glued to a clipboard. He flips a couple of pages and murmurs to himself. "Hmm. Can you come give me a hand? Might as well restock the neural growth hormones, anabolic steroids, antibiotics, and Neurotoxin A16. We're low on them all." I nod. He ambles in the direction of the elevator, still buried in the clipboard.

"Neurotoxin A16? Which one is that?" I say, as the elevator descends.

"It's the protein which causes selective necrosis of the amygdala, by blocking the transport of electrons during oxidative phosphorylation, which results in the cessation of production of ATP – no fuel, the cells cease to function – they suffocate, basically."

"And without an amygdala, the animals are much more docile, and easier to handle." I shrug. "Makes sense."

"Now, if we could only develop a selective neurotoxin for the periaqueductal grey matter, we might be able to stop the animals from screaming in pain all the time. Gets damn annoying real quick." Mason says. (We often bitch and commiserate about the ongoing irritations of the job.)

"Hey, why so complicated?" I say, flippantly. "We should just sever the spines of all the baby animals, when we take them out of the pickle jars. Just make 'em all tetraplegic, then they'd stop screaming *and* flailing. *Bonus!!!*"

He looks thoughtful. "Actually... that's a great idea! I'm going to look into that." His serious tone makes me uncomfortable, so I keep joking. "While we're at it, we can sew shut their anuses and urethras, so they don't stink so much!" I force a grin, but my words fall flat. Mason is away somewhere, considering, devising.

The elevator stops. The doors open. It looks totally different than the warehouse level containing hundreds of massive shelves of barrels, bottles, and boxes of chemicals. This is just a little hallway. The LED display above the door shows in red: ***SL4***

"Oh. Wrong floor," says Mason, reaching for the button.

"Wait," I say, "I've never been here before; what is this place?"

"Just more labs. We do original research to try to improve the living conditions for the citizens of New Genesis over future generations. It's actually the main funding initiative of NGFF: the food production aspect is merely a mundane necessity." Mason says listlessly, without looking up from the button panel, his arm still extended.

"Oh, wow. Can I have a look?" I ask, very interested.

"I guess so." He shrugs ambivalently.

We walk down the hall. The walls are cinder blocks painted white. The floor and ceiling is grey concrete. A continuous line of fluorescent tubes travels down the center of the ceiling, flickering and buzzing. Our footsteps sound gargantuan as the reverberating sound waves bounce around us.

The first door we come to is labelled *SL4-Abnormal Development Experimental Research Lab-01:* Mason presses the button to open the door, which slides open with a swish. The hallway before us is bright and antiseptic, almost cheerful in appearance. It branches to the left. From somewhere out of sight, I can hear strange noises: moans and groans, and other indescribable vocalizations. I look inquisitively over at Mason. He is spinning his lanyard on his finger as he walks listlessly down the hallway. I follow.

As we round the corner, my jaw drops.

It is a large, square room, blindingly white and clean. There are no guards or lab workers in sight. Around the room are cages, like the ones in the animal labs upstairs. But these ones are filled with... *human children!* They are all naked, and utterly hideous to behold.

One boy has no eyes or nose, just a mouth hovering beneath a flat, blank wall of skin, as if he were a child's doll which somehow made it off the production line without having all its features painted on. I shudder. I recognize some of these mutations from studies in university, of the fallout after the Event. A small child of indeterminate sex is covered in scabby scales, with nothing resembling skin whatsoever. *Lamellar Ichthyosis...* I whisper the words breathlessly.

A girl who can't be more than three is lying on her back in one of the cages. Her head is swollen to five or six times the normal size, like the old illustrations of aliens. *Hydrocephalus.* Her eyes are tiny and beady, and are nearly rolled all the way back into her head. Her scalp is bald, and covered with bulging blue veins. Her breath scrapes her throat on the way out, and frothy spittle bubbles from between her pale lips. Her arms are twitching in seemingly random motions.

One child has four arms and four legs. *Polymelia.* Another looks perfectly normal, except an extra head grows from her own, crown to crown. This extra head can move its eyes and lips independently, but has no body other than a lump of an upper torso. *A parasitic twin!* A little baby with her heart protruding from her body. *Ectopia Cordis.*

In one corner of the room is a pile of little bodies, obviously dead. A baby with bulging blood-red eyes and swollen lips, white skin, and jagged red lighting branches all over its body. *Harlequin-Type Ichthyosis.* A baby with no skin at all. *Epidermolysis Bullosa.* A grotesque creature with no neck, a fat body and massive protruding frog-like eyes, still open. It is missing the top of its skull, and the exposed brain so severely underdeveloped, had it survived, it would only have been able to perform basic autonomic functions – no sensory perception or thinking. *Anencephaly.*

I feel like I'm going to vomit. Sure, I've studied these conditions, but at that point, the educational images were still and silent. Here and now, these poor children are making the most pitiful of noises; it is so much more *real* than the textbooks. Suddenly, I startle at the sound of terrified, agonized screams flooding from the adjoining room. I look in bewildered terror at Mason, but he is busy trimming his fingernails with a utility blade. I hurry over and impatiently punch the button to open the door.

The room is small and sterile. It reminds me of a dentist's office. In the center of the room, in a large reclining medical chair, beneath a bank of lights, sits a small boy of around seven years of age. His face is massive, and appears melted, as if he were made of wax and ventured too close to a candle. *Neurofibromatosis!* I gasp.

The chair is surrounded by computer banks with indecipherable readouts, and trolleys laden with tools and instruments. A man in a white coat is vivisecting the child, *cutting open his face*, while the boy, bound at wrists, ankles, and forehead, is shrieking and crying hysterically. The shocking scene before me is so repellent I nearly gag. Without thinking, I cry out:

"What the fuck are you doing?!" My voice sounds pathetically small, shrill, and girlish.

The guy startles so badly he cuts his own hand open, a deep gash which immediately begins gushing blood. "Fuck me!" he yells, dropping the scalpel and clutching the wound with his other hand. He glares at me.

"Christ, lady! Are you nuts? Look what you made me do! Jesus H!!" He turns and rushes out of a far door, bleeding all over the place and cursing. Mason is staring at me obscenely.

"Dude, what the fuck is *wrong* with you?!" he hisses scornfully, his face a portrait of ridicule. *Me?!* I drop my jaw. I'm speechless; I don't even know what to say to that, so I just turn and run over to the boy.

"Where are your mommy and daddy?" I ask, but the terrified child just stares at me, bewildered.

"Look, just stay here, okay? I'll come back with help!" I try to reassure the kid, then practically run back to the elevator. Mason chases after me, protesting.

"Would you just *stop?!* You're going to get us both written up!! What is your *problem?!*" he hollers breathlessly. The elevator doors close before he catches up to me.

I repeatedly stab the button for **SL1:** The Medical Bay. However, instead of going up, the elevator goes down! Someone must have already called it a moment before. The doors open at **SL5,** and a scientist steps on, absorbed in something on a clipboard. I try to disguise my distress from him, and I am about to press the door close button, when something odd catches my eye.

The first door in this hallway is marked *SL5-01 – Spawn Gestation Chamber 1A.* I just saw a scientist carrying a pickle jar in there, with something inside it that made me take a second glance, but by the time I looked back it had disappeared around the corner. I scramble out of the elevator and chase after him, but once inside, I just spin in circles, stupefied. It is a room identical to the ones I work in upstairs, but each of these thousands of jars holds a tiny, developing human foetus. A handful of scientists are working away quietly. I recognize many of them. *What the hell is going on in this place?!*

I wheel around and storm back to the elevator. It is busy. I descend the stairs two at a time, plunging deeper into the fetid bowels of this farmhouse of horrors.

...

SL6 is dead quiet.

"Quality Protein-Rich Meat Products"

The entire level is a massive, octagonal amphitheater. In the center is an operating table, lit from above by three bright lamps. Various surgical tools and medical equipment surround it. The seats of the amphitheater are dark; in the blinding light of the stage, I can't see. I step closer, and jump in fright.

Thousands of humans are standing in the bleachers, silently watching me. There are at least a hundred rows, and the octagon, at its narrowest circumference, seats at least four hundred people.

"Who the fuck are you people?!" I scream. They do not respond. I walk towards them. As I approach one of the ghosts, I yell at it. I bluff, telling it I have a proton pistol in my pocket and I will blow it the fuck away if it does not answer me. It does not answer me. Any sentient person would think twice before inviting an proton blast. *Perhaps it is not a person after all?*

All I can see is a dark humanoid figure against a white rectangular background, silent and still. A single red light shines out of the darkness beside it. My most basic instinct is to push it, so I do, even against my better judgment. It turns green, and a moment later, a bright light floods the humanoid from above. I squint in the painful illumination, and when I can see again, I gasp. It is a woman!

She is completely naked, bound to a vertical board by clamps extending like insect legs over her body, pinning everything except for her lower ventromedial torso, which is bisected down the center by a strange line, like she's been partially cut in half but then stuck back together.

I am startled to see her chest moving. *She is alive!* I look at her face. Her eyes are open, but glazed over. A respiration mask is strapped to her mouth. Her arms are perforated with multiple IV lines. A urethral catheter protrudes from her genitals, and an enema tube snakes out from behind.

I move to the next figure along the line and press the button. Another woman. The next: another, and another, and another. *What is going on here?* I want to release them, but I don't know how. I see a button with a rectangle beneath an arrow pointing UP, so I take a guess, and push it. A horizontal strip of digital text appears, in red, seven-segmented LED lights, like a bedside alarm clock. The text scrolls from right to left:

[SPAWNMOTHER #3490, ENGAGE OPERATION]

I hear the whine of hydraulics, and, alarmed, I step back. From high in the theater, a crane arm snakes down, and a massive clamp takes a firm hold of the board the woman is clasped to. With a hiss, all tubes (IV, catheter, and enema) disengage from detachable junctions close to their insertion point, simultaneously. The hydraulic arm lifts the bound woman up into the air. It swivels, rotates, and places the unit horizontally on the operating table in the center of the stage. I run over to it. A digital display at this station has

"Quality Protein-Rich Meat Products"

activated. A similar strip of text appears:

[AUTOMATION ENGAGED: PREPARING SPAWNMOTHER FOR FOETAL EXTRACTION]

Before my horrified eyes, another hydraulic arm swivels down, and, with a laser, cuts along a pre-existing line, just below the navel, while two other arms pry the flesh apart laterally, revealing her abdominal cavity.

[FOETAL EXTRACTION PROCEDURE INITIATED]

I can only stare as the laser slices open this nameless woman's womb along a partially healed scar, and opens this up like a purse. By the light above, I can see a tiny undeveloped human inside. *It is sucking its thumb.* The text display is blinking insistently:

[URGENT: MANUALLY REMOVE FOETUS IMMEDIATELY]
[URGENT: MANUALLY REMOVE FOETUS IMMEDIATELY]
[URGENT: MANUALLY REMOVE FOETUS IMMEDIATELY]

I can't move.
I can't think.
I can't breathe.

I startle as suddenly I hear Mason's voice in my right ear: "Percy, what are you doing here?! Look, we really need to get back to work. We have to have that bovine serum ready for tonight's batch."

I whirl on him, incensed. "You *knew* about this, didn't you?!" I spit the words at him like venom.

"Well, yeah. I worked on *SL5* and down here for a couple years, until you showed up, then I was reassigned to train you." His voice is deadpan, matter-of-fact, and he even seems a little bewildered at my aggressive demeanour.

"*You* **WHAT?!**" I yell in his face.

"Jesus Christ...What's your problem, Persephone?" he says peevishly, stepping back.

"What's my *problem?* You sick fuck! You're farming *people!!*" I can feel my neck burning. My fists are clenched and trembling.

"So? We've been doing this for years! Tomakin developed the procedure. He has probably single-handedly saved mankind," he says, nonchalantly, as he lights an ersatz cigarette and exhales a thick cloud of smoke, which makes me gag.

"Quality Protein-Rich Meat Products"

"What would the citizens of New Genesis say if they knew about this? It's completely immoral!" I'm so worked up I'm shaking all over.

He shrugs. "Most people *do* know about it. It's no secret. Sure, it's brutal, but as long as it doesn't interrupt their holovision and their meat rations, they're happy to ignore it. But you're missing the entire point here. It's a *good* thing!!" he insists.

"Think about it! *Genetic modification!!*" he exclaims, gesticulating animatedly, the cigarette painting swirls of trailing smoke in the air. "This is cutting edge science! Surely you of all people must appreciate that! The benefits are indisputable! The fact is, New Genesis has two severe problems, which are directly caused by its citizens, but those same citizens refuse to address them. Therefore, we must take action for them, since they are obviously too stupid to realize they are causing the internal collapse of our new civilization.

"The first problem is food: supply and demand. The privileged, ignorant consumers of New Genesis eat more than twice the amount necessary to sustain them. This behaviour is completely unsustainable. Our resources are taxed as they are, production is decreasing, and demand is increasing. It is doing so because of the second problem: rampant overpopulation. The only things these imbecilic primates are good at is eating and fucking and popping out babies like an automated production line."

With only so much as a cursory glance, Mason casually reaches over and ashes his cigarette into the open womb of *SpawnMother #3490*.

"The truth is, humanity is literally a cancer upon the planet: it grows without check, without density-dependent inhibition, irrespective of available resources, and it will do so until it kills its host: Earth. However, we have found and initiated solutions to these problems. You may recall some months ago a bill was passed mandating every new pregnancy be genetically screened for diseases, foreseeable disabilities, etc. We knock out the prospective mothers with harmless gas, and perform this screening, which, in reality, is just a placental fluid test, but we also perform an invasive surgery via the vagina – which leaves no evidence of surgery, so the mother never realizes a thing – wherein we extend a tiny hypodermic needle up through the cervix and into the womb. We then selectively inject trillions of copies of one of two different viruses into the foetus, which spreads a modified RNA sequence throughout its body, attacking, in particular, its active stem cells. This introduces two important genetic modifications into the embryonic development of the new population:

1. Each new person born will have only $1/3^{rd}$ of the appetite they would normally.
2. Nineteen of every twenty new citizens will have no sex drive whatsoever.

"Quality Protein-Rich Meat Products"

In this way, we will eventually end up with a surplus of food, and only 5% of the population reproducing. Both problems solved! We are currently working on some of the more secondary issues – for example, not making people smarter, as might seem intuitive, but making them more placid and pliable. Smart people cause problems for governments. A functionally retarded population is most manageable." He shows me his yellow teeth.

"But why all this?!" I hiss, "Why not just use somatic cell nuclear transfer, and spare the lives of these women?"

"Surely you can't be serious?? In order to have the most benefit, we need to work with unique human subjects. Working with clones will get us nowhere: each foetus we use must be genetically distinct, the product of meiosis, and a natural embryonic development. So, we use live mothers. We – that is, myself and the other guys – we *personally* impregnate the women, then wait until the appropriate stage of development – whatever developmental level we want to study; usually we have a few tiers dedicated to several significant points along the timeline – before removing the foetus. We then fuse the womb shut, chemically induce ovulation, and the process is then begun again. This way we can get about five foetuses a year per SpawnMother. We currently have about 9,000 SpawnMothers, so we burn through about 45,000 foetuses per year in our research. I must say, we make excellent progress."

I grab Mason by his lab coat and pull him very close, snarling through my teeth at him. "These are *real women* you are using as foetus production factories! *Real children* whose only life is one of pain and torture! They are *living beings!* They don't deserve this savage treatment!"

He pushes me away, scowling, smoothing the lapels of his lab coat.

"Don't be naïve, Percy. Developing these solutions is a tedious business, and most attempts are failures. We must press on and learn new ways to improve the citizens of tomorrow. Sure, we're using live women, but they're merely RPs. There is more than one way to be RePurposed, and, in the long run, this is even more productive to humanity than the mulching factory. And the babies aren't even human – they're not given the chance to be – there's no loss there. They can't even be considered collateral damage."

Mason presses a series of buttons on the terminal. The mechanical arms sew the womb back up, sealing the fate of the tiny human inside. Then it stitches the belly of the woman, before replacing the unit back into the rows of faceless others. The lights again go dark.

"Besides," he says to me. "You stand here, raving your head off at me, yet you have more than happily contributed to the torture of *millions* of animals during your time here. Are they not living beings, too?" He flashes me an unambiguous look, then turns and begins walking to the elevator, a rectangle of light in the darkness. "Now come on; we really need to get back to work." he calls over his shoulder.

"Quality Protein-Rich Meat Products"

I stand there, in the darkness. Ahead of me, the warm light of the elevator spills out over the floor, almost to my toes. I turn and look back into the pitch black womb of the amphitheater, to the SpawnMothers. Their breathing machines produce 10,000 dry, rasping whispers. It sounds as if they're *accusing* me!!!

"*Look,*" I want to tell them, *"I'm just doing my job!!!"* From the darkness, I see them all staring at me, unmollified.

I shudder and turn back around. Mason stands in the elevator, waiting. At the end of the day he'll go home to his fancy New Society apartment, with his full-size gaming holofield... and I'll go home to the OS projects.... I sigh and stare at my feet. My shoe is untied. How did I not notice that when I was running? I bend down and mechanically perform the sequential loops.

I... I should think rationally about this... The truth is, I'm *almost there!!* In just a few more months I'll have saved enough to afford the exorbitant application fee for NS citizenship, then I'll be able to upgrade to a better apartment, and soon, I'll install my **own** gaming holofield, **bigger and better** than Mason's... It'll have 24 surround-speakers, not just 12, and a 24-bit profile of **16,777,216** colours, instead of only 12-bit!! I'll have him over and tell my kitchen to make him a drink. (See, he doesn't even have an automatic kitchen.) And I'll have an antigravity bed, too, with the walls configured to display an ocean sunrise when I wake up. I chuckle inwardly: I can't wait to see the look on Mason's face when he sees it all; he'll be *so* jealous!

Suddenly, I realize that for the first time in months, I have a tangible craving for bacon. Strange.

[2015-12-22 / 02:26:01]

Earthship : Devolution

"Well?"

"I hate to say it, but it's true. The starboard thruster is malfunctioning. I pulled up the activity logs for the past week and ran the correlation with the command logs for the control system. The Pearson r coefficient was 0.06."

"Strange. If it were negative I would understand it – the thruster just wouldn't be responding – but why so close to neutral, and positive?"

"I wondered that myself, so I looked into the data. Turns out the thruster does/doesn't fire according to bridge command some of the time, but it also fires almost as frequently when we haven't even directed it to. So the correlation pretty much cancels itself out."

"Damn." Ezra Kolby chewed his thumbnail and furrowed his brow. "Damn! We've gotta get this shipment to *Omega-2-Alpha* within a fortnight, and we've already drifted two parsecs off course... Blast! It's impossible!" He stood up from the computer terminal he had been working on, strode over to the shuttle wall, and pushed a button. Whirring mechanically, the covering of the broad viewing port slid up and into the ceiling, revealing a picturesque window twenty feet long and seven feet high. Kolby stared out into the infinite blackness of space. He could see nothing familiar. The view was studded with stars, as usual, but none of the constellations he was accustomed to seeing were there. It was disturbing. They were postal workers, not deep-space adventurers! He cursed aloud, and resumed biting his fingernails.

"Look, don't worry about it man." Mirokov Vasilyev Ivanovic said, coming up to stand beside his shipmate. "So we'll be late. It's not the end of the world. I'll call it in, then run an electronics diagnostic to see if I can't narrow down the source of the issue. It might even be an easy repair, honestly. It sounds to me like a loose wire."

He smiled and clapped Kolby on the back heartily, then walked out of the room. Kolby sighed with irritation. He really didn't know how the Russian could afford to be so *optimistic* all the time. But they'd been partners for nearly seven years. Miro was the happy-go-lucky and devil-may-care half of the pair; Kolby was chronically stressed and congenitally uptight. They kind of balanced each other out. He sat back down at the desk and resumed his work re-plotting their trajectory to get themselves back on course. Of course, he'd have to wait until they sorted through this issue with the thruster – no sense attempting to change course, just to be pushed away again. But, he could still get their bearings and do a tentative calculation to get a broad idea of the shape of things.

Ezra Kolby was a thin man in his late thirties. He wore round spectacles and had short brown hair and brown eyes. Altogether, he wasn't much to look at, but hey, out in space, there's nobody to look good for, so who cares, right?

He was the navigator and accountant in the business he and Miro had set up years back when they got out of college. They called themselves *RockHopper Interstellar Courier Service,* or, rather, Mirokov had called them "The RockHoppers", since they went from planet to planet, but Kolby puckered his face and opted for the more conservative "K&I Interstellar Courier Service". Obviously, they had reached a compromise.

Kolby handled the paperwork and the navigation because he excelled at calculus and trigonometry and spreadsheets. Mirokov was a few years older than Kolby. He took care of the Public Relations and sales, because he was a cheerful, smooth talker who seemed to like people, for some bizarre reason that didn't exist within Kolby. He was also the tech whiz of the two, so he handled computer issues and hardware repairs. He stood six foot six and was built like a tree trunk. Kolby was certain he could crush boulders with his bare hands.

He rubbed his tired eyes and went on a hunt for freeze-dried coffee crystals. He had just boiled the water and added sugar and whitener, when Mirokov entered the room, absorbed in something he was reading on his tablet.

"Look, look!" he said, groping blindly for Kolby's shoulder, without glancing up. "I'm certain I've found the source of the problem."

Kolby brushed his hand away petulantly, and stood by him, peering at the screen. He shouldn't have bothered; it was all Greek to him. "What am I looking at?" he asked drily.

"This is a schematic for the electrical pathways in the circuitry and wiring of the starboard thruster. On this view it looks like a confusing jumble of multi-coloured lines, but watch as I switch it to impedance view. See? Now almost all of the lines are dark blue: beneath 10 kilohms, but right here, this one is bright red, and the impedance reading is "--.--kΩ". That means it's immeasurable because there is a break in the circuit. Moreover, keep watching it for a second."

Kolby watched. After a few seconds of nothing happening, he noticed the red line suddenly flicker to blue, then green. After another few seconds, it went back to red. Miro explained.

"That means the connection is intermittent, and it's misinterpreting the signal as a command. When it turned green, the source was actively transmitting to the sink – the thruster was firing, uncommanded. Ten bucks says it's a loose wire. Totally easy fix. I'm going to suit up and go solder it."

"Damn!" Kolby exclaimed. "That's good news!" he laughed out loud, despite himself.

Earthship : Devolution

"Golly!!" hollered Miro, suddenly throwing his hands up and startling his partner. "It smiles! It even laughs!"

Kolby's grin instantly disappeared, and his face reformed into its customary sour look. Miro shoved his shoulder playfully, and jogged off down the corridor. Once he was gone, Kolby relaxed his face and smiled again. They had teased each other like this since they were kids, growing up together on the Earthship. He went back to his navigation work, in earnest this time.

A few minutes later, he heard Mirokov's voice crackling over the intercom. "Alright, I'm heading to the airlock. You got me?"

"I got you, pal." replied Kolby, wheeling his chair over to the bank of monitors displaying the various camera feeds. He pulled up onto the big screen the feed of the airlock. He saw Mirokov, even bulkier and larger than usual in his space suit, checking his oxygen tanks. Presently he looked up at the camera and gave a thumbs up. "Good to go."

"Opening airlock door." Kolby punched a button and the door slid open. Miro stepped through, and Kolby closed it behind him. "Opening hull door."
...

With a loud hiss, the external door slid up along the shell of the ship. Mirokov held onto the ceiling grip holds, as the atmosphere violently rushed out and the cold nothingness of space invaded the airlock. Presently, he released his grip and began floating. He gently swung out, pivoting on a handhold closer to the door. His body rotated upside down along hull of the ship. It took him a moment to get his orientation, or rather, to lose it. In space, down is wherever your feet are pointing.

He gripped the joysticks which extended from his jetpack, and, with small, short bursts, glided down the hull of the ship to the tailfin which housed the starboard thruster.

"You all good?" said Kolby's voice in his ear.

"Doin' just fine, pal."

"Okay, I'm going back to navigation. Holler if you need anything."

"Roger that." Miro located and opened the panel for the thruster's circuitry. After a few minutes of tinkering with an ohm meter, testing electrical resistance, he found the guilty wire. "Just as I thought," he muttered to himself.

"What was that?"

"Oh, nothing, just talking to myself. I was right; it's a loose wire. I'll be back in there in a jiffy."

"And how long, exactly, is a *"jiffy"*? I am unfamiliar with this unit of temporal measurement."

"Yeah, yeah. Ten minutes tops."

"Good to hear. Stay safe, buddy."

Miro reached into his side pouch and removed his soldering kit.

...

Kolby clicked off the radio mic and turned back to his work. Something was troubling him. According to the astronavigator, they were heading toward a planet. It was just a lifeless, uninhabited rock, but it was dense – it had collected four moons so far. If they ventured near it, they would be sucked into its orbit. He stood up and went to the observation window, and was dismayed to discover that he could even see the planet with his naked eye. According to their speed and trajectory, they would enter its gravitational field in fifteen minutes.

He gnawed on his thumbnail, and sat back down. They should be fine. Miro would be back before then. Even so, he needed to know. He reached for the transceiver.

...

"Miro, we're headed directly towards a planet; we have to shift course within fifteen minutes, or we'll be pulled into its gravitational field." Kolby's voice piped into Mirokov's helmet.

"Is that so? Okay, I'm just about to solder the wire now."

Working skilfully through awkward, bulky gloves, he carefully placed the tip of his iron onto the circuit, and was just about to touch the soldering wire to it, when the thruster suddenly fired. The wing lurched ahead as the ship rotated in space, and Miro incontinently rolled back along the hull, toward the huge engine. He activated the electromagnet in his glove and slammed it onto the hull just in time to avoid being barbecued.

"Shit, Ezra, what are you doing?!" he yelled into the comm.

"What!?"

"Don't try to shift course while I'm doing this, man!"

"I didn't do anything!"

"Shit! The thruster fired right as I was about to solder!" Miro began to sweat. It was still engaging at what seemed like full strength, only a few yards away. That was unusual. It had only been misfiring for mere centiseconds, before. Using his electromagnets, he pulled himself up the hull of the ship, back to the circuit board, then cursed when he saw what had happened. When the wing lurched, his soldering iron slipped and tore loose several wires and capacitors. The circuit board was a hot mess. What is worse, he had dropped his tools: he couldn't fix it now.

"Miro? Talk to me, man! We're careening directly towards that planet!!" squawked his helmet.

"The... it's wrecked! It's totally fucked, man! Look, just fire the port thrusters full-on, and don't stop, okay? I'm going to try to disable this engine."

"Damn! Okay!"

Mirokov stuck fast to the hull as Colby activated the opposite engine. After the initial jerk, the ship stabilized, and he got to work again. He pulled out his tablet and located the main I/O circuit – if he disabled that one, no power would get through to the engine, and it would stop. He looked up. He could see the planet fast approaching portside. Their trajectory had corrected so that they were no longer on a collision course, but they were in danger of heading into the upper atmosphere and burning up, if he didn't cut this engine *immediately*. Sweat was dripping into his eyes; he automatically reached up to mop his brow with his forearm and swore as it bounced off his helmet. With trembling hands, he found the wire and pulled it. To his infinite relief, the thruster quit firing. He shouted exultantly and collapsed against the hull, panting.

A moment later, Mirokov jetted back to the airlock. When he was safely inside, he threw off his gear. He was soaked with sweat and breathing heavily. He raced to the bridge, where Kolby was at the pilot's helm, staring anxiously out of the cockpit window.

"We're stuck in orbit..." he said, dazedly. "Look, the port thruster is going full blast, but we're merely spinning in place."

Miro looked. It was true. The planet was receding to the port side rapidly, but they were no further away from it. They had avoided a collision, and were out of danger of the atmosphere, but they were back to their original problem: they were now trapped within the gravitational field of the massive rock.

"You have to go back out there and reengage the engine so we can pull out of orbit!" cried Kolby, in a panic. He was paler than usual.

"It's no use..." Mirokov moaned lugubriously. "This is just a little merchant ship. Even with both thrusters engaged, we couldn't break free." He collapsed into a chair and hung his head dejectedly, leaning forward with his elbows on his knees and his face in his hands. It was the lowest Kolby had ever seen him.

"Well, look... we can figure it out," he said, without much conviction. Miro was silent. Kolby said nothing further, and went back to anxiously biting his nails. After a few minutes, Miro said something so quietly that Kolby had to ask him to repeat himself.

"I said, I've broken my promise to Ilya." (This was the name of Miro's seven-year-old daughter, back on Earthship.) "I promised her that when I got home I would teach her how to use a slingshot, you know, the old-fashioned leather sort with two strings and a pocket, that you whip around and release.

Earthship : Devolution

But I'll never get home, and she'll have to live her whole life wondering what happened to me!!!" he mourned, but Kolby had stopped listening.

"That's *PERFECT!*" he shouted triumphantly, startling Mirokov out of his morosity. "A slingshot! We'll use centrifugal force to escape!" Miro merely gaped. "We'll engage both thrusters, and fly *with* the orbit, faster and faster, until centrifugal force pushes us to the outer peripheries of the magnetic pull, where it is at its weakest! Then, we'll reverse the starboard thruster while maintaining full-forward on port, and use the change in momentum to break us out of orbit!" Kolby hopped out of his chair and began dancing and whooping triumphantly. Mirokov spent a moment envisioning it, then his countenance melted into a look of epiphany, and he launched out of his seat to join his partner. They linked arms and wheeled in circles. After a few seconds of this, they let go and collapsed onto the floor, dizzy and elated with hope. They sat there, against opposite walls, breathing heavily. Presently, they regained their composures.

"Ahem," said Kolby, suddenly looking as much a grumpy old man as ever. "Best get to it." he said, and brusquely turned and walked over to his desk, to resume his calculations. Mirokov fairly bounded over to the airlock and jumped back into his suit, to go reconnect the I/O circuit.

...

The little merchant ship built up speed until it was at maximum velocity. Then, Kolby quickly attempted to calculate the best moment to reverse the starboard thruster, so that they would break out of orbit without smashing into any of the planet's four moons. At what he hoped was the precise moment, he gave the order, and within the cockpit, Mirokov stabbed the button.

There was a strong jolt, and the ship rotated 75° clockwise. There was a moment of straining wherein they seemed not to move whatsoever, and the two men held their breath. For what seemed like eons, the ship edged incrementally away from the surface of the planet, then with another lurch, broke free of orbit, shooting away from the planet, spinning wildly, until Mirokov righted the starboard engine.

"Man, I wish we had some champagne!" he cried, turning to Kolby with a triumphant grin. But Kolby was not smiling. He was peering at a display, his brow furrowed more deeply than usual. Miro's expression turned to dismayal, and he looked over to see what was so troubling.

Beneath Kolby's anxiously tapping finger, Miro saw the fuel gauge. It was at 1%. He cursed. Of course! Space flight is supposed to use very little fuel: an initial speed is established, and since there is no atmosphere in space, there is no friction to slow a ship, so all that is needed is short bursts occasionally, to keep on track. On Earthship, astronauts don't face the problems of early space flight – that is, the challenge of using a vast amount of fuel merely to break out of Earth's atmosphere – because Earthship is a monolithic space ship/station which naturally has no atmosphere outside of its glass shell. However, fuel is voluminous, and for a small transport vehicle, most of the cargo space is, of course, used for cargo. Consequently, the *RockHopper* had just used up all of its fuel in its mad race around and away from the villainous, abducting planet.

At that moment, as if on cue, the engines died. The low rumble that been the background of their daily lives for seven years faded into a silence that smothered them until they felt like they couldn't breathe. Kolby pounded the wall with his fist and cursed loudly at the fates which would not give them one goddamned break. Mirokov merely stood there, glassy-eyed, his towering frame swaying slightly. His lips were moving, but no sound was forthcoming. Presently, he lay down on the floor and put his face in his hands.

"Fuck the champagne; I want some whiskey." he growled disconsolately.

"Dude, you don't even drink. But you're right, I'd go for that about now..." After a moment of silently watching him, Kolby turned away from Mirokov. It was disturbing to see his friend, who was usually so cheerful, in this dark, despairing state.

Not that there was any other way he should be expected to feel, now. They were already dead; all that was left was to wait for it to happen.

...

The two men decided that the best thing they could do right then was to get a good sleep, and a good breakfast, so they took turns: while one slept, the other kept an eye on the astrochart. The plain truth was that they had broken out of orbit at a nearly inconceivable velocity, and, with nothing to slow them down, they hurtled through the vast emptiness of space at about 1/3 the speed of light. The best they could do was hope they didn't crash into anything. In theory, there was not even any reason for someone to keep lookout, because even if they were to find themselves on a collision course, there was nothing they could do about it. However, they both knew that neither of them could sleep knowing they were blindly careening into a great unknown. They preferred to look death in the eye, rather than have it blindside them. (Neither of them wished to acknowledge the glaring fact that, at that velocity, even a piece of space debris the size of a grain of sand would tear the craft apart.)

Six weeks later, they were still moving, just as fast as ever. They were now completely off the star charts. They had radioed back to Earthship at the beginning, to report the disaster, and were told to sit tight: help was on the way. Miro had a mini celebration with an extra spoonful of sugar in his coffee, but Kolby sat moodily by the viewing port, staring out at the crushing darkness, perforated by so many tiny pinpoints of light. For the first time, the stars which he had found so fascinating and beautiful now revealed themselves for what they were: inconceivably massive raging storms of combusting gases surrounded by a merciless vacuum of nothingness. Infinite heat surrounded by infinite cold. *Death surrounded by death.*

Kolby knew that Earthship was merely placating them. Of course nobody would be dispatched all the way into the middle of nothing and nowhere, just to rescue an insignificant merchant ship with a juvenile company name. He looked bitterly over at Mirokov, who was sitting in his bunk, sipping his coffee daintily and looking like a blissful cat in a ray of sunshine. He felt angrier by the second; he knew that Mirokov knew they would never again see Earthship. He had a fierce urge to storm over there, grab that damned coffee cup out of Miro's fool hand, and smash it against the wall, and scream, "*What right do you have to be so happy?*"

...

Hurtling through uncharted space, Kolby had never felt more alone, or more terrified. He felt like he had when he was just a little boy, and he got lost in the commercial districts of Earthship. He had wandered off, chasing a mechanical puppy with strobing neon lights for fur, and spent what felt like days bawling and frantically searching for his assigned caregiver. In reality, it was only about an hour he was separated from her, and half of that was spent in the care of a kind old shopkeeper who smelled like curry and onions and kept trying to cheer him up with a decadently painted set of Russian *Matryoshka* Nesting Dolls, but it was an experience of helplessness and isolation he had never forgotten. He felt like that presently, and with every passing day was less inclined to observe the staunch cultural standards of reserved politeness, never showing one's feelings.

"Why are we even sustaining ourselves?" he asked bitterly, one mealtime, pushing away his "stimulated-chicken-flavoured" bean curd protein mash in revulsion. "We're just drawing out the inevitable. We're going to **die**, Miro, and there's nothing we can do about it, so why are we prolonging it?"

Mirokov put down the can of beans he had been eating, and smiled, patting his belly as he leaned back in his chair. "Because we're not dead *yet*, Ezra, and until that day comes, these are some damn good vittles!" Seeing Kolby incredulously staring a hole through his head, he assumed a more serious tone.

"Okay, look... Let us assume you are correct, and we are heading to our imminent doom – which, I may add, is not a certainty, because *nothing* is ever certain – you cannot deny that, in this moment, we are not yet dead. Why, then, would you make yourself miserable by acting as if you already were? If it is inevitable, you might as well enjoy every minute up until that point, because it will come regardless of whether you are happy or horrid of mood."

"Pfft. Yeah right. What about your wife – what about Polina?? How can you justify being vapidly happy, eating your fucking beans, when you know perfectly well the anguished heartbreak and grief she's experiencing?" Kolby snapped, then added, as an extra cruel needling, "What about Ilya? Have you already forgotten how she'll grow up bereft, without a father?" A ghost of an expression, distant and sorrowful, drifted across Mirokov's countenance, and he turned away for a moment. When he looked back, his eyes were wet. Kolby was surprised to find himself actually sorry he had mentioned it.

Miro sighed, and looked dolefully at him.. "Ezra... *What is death?*" he asked, cryptically. "To you it may be ceasing to occupy a definitive space in the universe, the failure to breathe, the termination of the heartbeat." He paused and looked away for a moment. "...To me, death is the incontrovertible admission that my loved ones and I will never see each other again. Yet, whilst I still breathe, there is always a chance that something unexpected may occur, and I'll find myself back home, scooping Ilya up into my arms. When my blood no longer runs through my veins, it becomes a truth, but until that moment... *I live.*"

"So a man can be alive and functioning, but still dead, if he has nobody who loves him..." Kolby mumbled, staring through his plate. Mirokov nodded his concurrence.

Kolby poked at his bean curd paste, and fell to silence.

...

"Miro, come here a minute, wouldja?" Kolby was in the cockpit, peering into the blackness of space ahead of them. He had the odd conviction that it seemed just a little blacker than usual. Mirokov appeared behind him. "Look straight ahead of us. What do you see?"

"... Nothing." said Miro, after a lengthy inspection of the universe before them.

"That's just it..." said Kolby, bemusedly. "There's *nothing* there. Oughtn't there be?" He scratched his thick beard. They had been drifting now for just over four months, and had long since run out of basics like razors and shaving cream, not to mention toilet paper and soap. He felt thoroughly vulgar.

"I suppose so," agreed Mirokov, "The star field usually tends to be more or less homogenously populated, and I seriously doubt we've reached the *end of the universe*, if there is such a thing."

"Listen, we have an X-Ray lens, right? Let's have a look at that nothingness."

He pulled it up on the big screen. The lens showed X-Rays colour-coded with respect to intensity. It was as he suspected: There were a few blue dots around the periphery of the screen, which corresponded to the stars visible to the edges of the cockpit's field of view, but in the middle, where there was nothing but blackness, the screen showed a searing white point in the center ringed with colours radiating outwards in the order of red, orange, yellow, green, then blue. On the scale, white was the maximum level which could be sensed, and blue was the minimum.

"We're heading straight into a massive black hole..." he breathed. Mirokov said nothing.

...

It was another five months before the little ship fell into the gravitational void. First, they became caught in its orbit, and so the whole time, they were spinning round the center point. Every day, however, they were moving closer to the obsidian mass of nothingness, like a rowboat caught in the pull of a large ocean maelstrom, spiralling down into its ominous, murky cavity. The time they spent caught in the vortex was one of conflicting emotions between the shipmates. Kolby became more moody and withdrawn, while Mirokov became more jovial and exuberant.

"Isn't this magnificent!" he cried, "We get to experience something nobody else has ever experienced before! I bet astronomical scientists would be so jealous of us right now!"

"I'm sure we're not the first, but nobody else has ever made it back with their observations." Kolby seethed irritably. He suddenly lashed out at Mirokov in a burst of resentment and pique. "What kind of nonsense are you spouting, anyhow? You're a damned fool! Think of the physics! There is no "other side", and there is no returning, because there will be nothing left to return. It is a *gravitational sinkhole,* so powerful that not even light can escape! *Light!* Do you even comprehend what that means?! When we get to the center of that thing, every atom in our bodies will be ripped to shreds! Electrons, protons, and neutrons, all torn asunder! We will be **terminated!!**" He was screaming at the other man, spittle accumulating on his unruly moustache and beard.

Mirokov bristled, and quite unexpectedly retaliated. "Don't call me a goddamned fool, Ezra!! You think I don't know all that?! But if I spent my time thinking about it, I'd be sick with fear, a miserable little wretch like *you* are! I'd rather think fancifully about what *might* happen, and at least enjoy the thought of some grand, supernatural adventure! Just leave me be!"

He stormed off to his cabin and slammed the door.

...

The two men awoke one morning to find the overhead lights flickering spasmodically. The pictures on the computer monitors were stretched and distorted. The equipment lights on the bridge control panel flashed like a carnival at night. Much later, there was a definitive point when everything died abruptly, as a flash of static electricity crackled and swarmed over the interior of the ship. Blinding white fingers of crepitating lightning crawled

Earthship : Devolution

and leapt over the electrical panels and the walls. Kolby and Miro sat in the darkness, staring silently out of the cockpit window. The blackness within was equal to that without: there was no light whatsoever. The two men sat side by side, but could not see each other, or even their own hands an inch away from their faces.

It has begun.

The hull of the ship began to moan and wail hauntingly, as if it were being slowly tortured to death. Indeed, the men were certain they could feel the floor shifting beneath them; they could hear the walls and ceilings moving and creaking around them. They jumped as they heard a sound like gunfire. Rivets were exploding from the hull under the immense pressure. Despite himself, Kolby lunged and clutched at Mirokov through the absolute blackness, in abject terror. He felt the large arms of his friend calmly reach over and hold him gently. This was no time for masculine macho-posturing. At that moment, they were merely two tiny humans in the grip of an unfathomably cold, black vortex of astronomical emptiness.

The sorrowful, ghoulish moaning and wailing of their poor little ship increased. Kolby felt as if it were alive, and was certain it was about to be torn apart. Their bodies would be sucked out into the blackness of space; their lungs, stomach, and intestines would implode in response to the negative pressure produced by the air being instantaneously sucked out by the vacuum. He shivered as the thought of it.

Gradually, the cabin became illuminated with a strange light. It was as if the aurora borealis had appeared around them: the entire visible spectrum of colours swam and swirled around them in a wispy, gossamer mist. Occasionally, it strobed dazzlingly, like a storm cloud within which lightning has just flashed. In the eerie light, Kolby could see his friend looking around, his jaw agape. His expression was one of astonishment and wonder, like a child at a fireworks show.

Before Kolby's eyes, Mirokov's face began to warp and shift. Like candy taffy, it pulled and tugged in one direction, then another. One moment, his head was three feet wide, his eyes horrendously elongated ovals, his mouth a vast horizontal slit. The next moment, it was being stretched diagonally, with an equally grotesque effect. He wondered if the same thing was happening to him, so he raised his hand in front of his face. He saw his fingers, as long as his forearm, wriggling like worms, and, horrified, immediately retracted it from sight. He gagged, feeling bile rise within his throat.

A thought occurred to him: The colours, the distortion, was it all a hallucination? Our bodies and brains are electrical machines, and electricity has a direct relationship to magnetism. Was the gravity of the black hole polarizing their internal magnetic field, resulting in these perceptual distortions? He had no idea. Looking around the interior of the ship, the

Earthship : Devolution

contortion appeared to be affecting everything. It was as if geometry and the constraints of physics had no place within reality anymore.

In the next moment, Kolby was overcome with a nauseatingly giddy sensation of vertigo. He had the sensation of rapidly spinning in a tumble dryer: one moment everything was upright, then it was upside down or sideways – orientation had no constant any longer. The swerving spinning grew to such intensity that Kolby was certain his head was about to be ripped apart at a molecular level. Before he blacked out, he reflected, with irony, that this was probably exactly what was happening.

...

He regained consciousness to find Mirokov kneeling over him, shaking him gently on his shoulder.

"...wake up, pal! Ezra! *Wake up!!"*

"Huh? What?" he mumbled groggily, sitting up and clutching his pounding head. "What's going on? I dreamed we actually went through that black hole..." It had seemed so real, but, no, of course they were still drifting aimlessly through space, circling that dark monster.

"Um, yeah, me too," said Mirokov, in a strange tone. "Buddy, I think we actually *did."*

"*What?!"* Kolby hollered, bolting upright. He bounded to his feet and stumbled to the window. He could see stars, which was unusual in itself since they happened upon the vortex, but what was even more bizarre is that he *recognized* them. These were constellations he had spent countless hours staring up into, as a kid growing up under the clear glassy shell of Earthship, and seeing them, in that moment, it really was heaven. He scrambled over to the astrochart and switched it on. To his extreme relief, it functioned perfectly. He also noticed that the lights had come back on.

Have we really had the same dream? Why has our position changed so drastically?

He pushed these questions out of his mind and focused on the star map. There, amidst a myriad of glowing stars of beautifully familiar configurations, a white dot glowed. It was their ship. Not far away, a much larger white dot gently pulsed.

Kolby ran over to the starboard viewing window and punched the button. It opened quietly. Before them loomed the incredibly massive bulk of the Earthship, only about 250 miles away. It was a great sphere, about 1/16th of the size of the original Earth, but still phenomenally monolithic. The entire outer surface was composed of clear, glasslike material which was strong enough to withstand the extreme cold, and the merciless vacuum, of space. Just like Earth, the globe rotated upon a tilted axis as it orbited the sun. This simulated day/night and the four seasons reasonably well.

Miro was already at the radio, calling for confirmation from Earthship's spaceport. There was no response. He tried several more times. Nothing.

"Huh. The radio must be broken. Well, we'll wait here, and soon there will be marines dispatched to determine why we are apparently not responding to them. We just have to sit tight."

...

They sat tight for a whole day, but still nobody came. It was certainly odd. At long last, Mirokov announced that they should go in and dock.

"How can we, with no fuel?"

"You forget about the orbital stations!"

Drifting in orbit around Earthship were several fuelling satellites accessible only to merchant and military ships. Kolby had indeed forgotten about those. He looked at the radar. There was actually one within two miles of their position. Mirokov explained that they could use their tractor beam to pull them to the station, where they could refuel. The starboard engine was still stuck in a full-thrust state, so Mirokov would have to go out to the circuit board again and manually control it by contacting the I/O wire to the circuit, by hand. As Kolby controlled the port engine and steered from inside, he would be constantly relaying instructions to Miro about when to engage/disengage his thruster.

They managed this with relatively little difficulty: since in-flight alterations of trajectory only need minor bursts, there was not an awful lot Miro had to do, as he waited, stuck to the hull by the electromagnets on his feet and left hand. The two spacemen were dying to see some other humans besides each other – having become obscene and vulgar spectacles by that point – but the fuelling stations were unmanned.

They had run short of food about three weeks prior, and had both lost a great deal of weight; it was most apparent on Mirokov. Their clothes were filthy and fit them like garbage bags. A shower would be most welcome. Miro was looking forward to seeing his family.

For some bizarre reason, Earthship's docking bay had been left wide open, which was lucky for them, since they couldn't radio in to ask for access, but it was definitely unusual. As a result, they were forced to exit the ship in full space gear. The moment he set foot on the landing pad, Kolby prostrated himself and hugged the tarmac. Then he got up and jumped for joy. *Waaay* up. Mirokov had to help him down with his jetpack, then flew them both up to the launch bay airlock.

Looking into the window of the control room, Kolby startled, his breath catching in his throat. Right next to the door, a woman was looking at him. *Staring*, actually. She stood there, without moving an inch, not even blinking. It creeped him out.

He knew he probably looked pretty ape-like beneath his helmet, on account of his huge, unruly whiskers, but it was just plain *rude* to stare like that! He quickly opened the door and stepped inside. The airlock was empty, but there were internal controls for pressure equalization and door function, so they let themselves in and ducked immediately into the locker room, ignoring the people they saw standing around in the spaceport. Kolby was hit again with a nagging feeling that something was *wrong*. It was *never* that quiet there. Everyone was always moving, always late for something. Even so, the two men were so relieved and overwhelmed to be home, they were practically bouncing, and literally giddy.

The first thing Miro did was access the telephone in the locker room to call his family. He waited, twirling the cable around his finger anxiously, but after nearly two minutes of silently moving his lips in a pleading prayer, he hung the phone up, crestfallen. Kolby gave him a friendly squeeze of his shoulder.

"Hey, don't feel bad, pal, look at the clock there; it's the middle of the day. Polina is probably out and about, and Ilya is at school. Just think, you will be waiting for them when they get home! Won't that be a surprise!"

"Hey, *yeah!*" exclaimed Miro, suddenly as excited as he was downtrodden a moment before. Then he frowned. He peered up at the wall clock and walked over to it. "Hey, this clock's busted, man." Sure enough, the second hand was holding perfectly immobile.

"Well, let's just get you home, anyway."

...

After a refreshing shower, during which they laughed and cajoled, the two men shaved, brushed their hair, and got dressed in fresh uniforms which they borrowed from the temp shelf, supplied for people who needed a quick change right away, so they could get home without wandering around Earthship in their space suits.

They stepped out into the spaceport, refreshed and in high spirits. Kolby wanted desperately to get a drink at the bar, but Miro just wanted to see his wife and daughter. As they walked into the cavernous commercial lobby, Kolby scowled at Miro in confusion. Everybody was still just standing around, like statues. As he approached a man, Kolby noticed that he was frozen mid-step. *Strange...*

He said hullo to the man, and even waved a hand in front of his eyes, but there was no response; the guy just kept staring forward, absurdly balanced on the toes of his left foot which was angled back behind him, while extending his right foot forward. His center of gravity was completely off-kilter. Even a tightrope walker couldn't balance in such a pose: *it defies physics!*

Then, from a few yards away, Mirokov called him over to a large planter pot housing a giant fern. A child was jumping off it to the ground, but he, too, was frozen, suspended in the air. It was as if somebody had paused a video right at that moment. Both men were bewildered.

What is going on??

Every single person in the spaceport appeared to be frozen in time. The same applied when they stepped outdoors into the city. Cars were paused on the freeway, flies hovered unmoving in the air, a cat was found in mid-bound towards a frightened rat, its claws outstretched, jaw open, its sharp fangs glistening in the sun.

Kolby stood up from where he had been bent inspecting this. He shook his head slowly. He had just decided he was still in bed on the shuttle, experiencing a horrible dream, so he had better not take it too seriously. Behind him, Mirokov was white in the face; abruptly he broke into a frantic run. Kolby ran after him, shouting at him. When the large man stopped, out of breath and weary of malnutrition, Kolby caught up to him and accosted him.

"What are you *doing*, man?!"

"Going to... my family!!" he said, breathlessly.

"Well, yeah, but we can't run there; let's take a cab."

"Oh, and who'll drive it?"

"Ohhh... uhh ... we will." Kolby said, walking over to the nearest absurdly-stationary vehicle and opening the door. He pried the driver out and dragged him heavily onto the sidewalk, still in a sitting configuration, his left hand raised as if on a steering wheel, his right hand holding a phone to his ear, and one foot extended, depressing some imaginary pedal. "Sorry about this, pal."

They drove to Mirokov's house. It took them a long time to get to their destination, because every road had turned into the world's worst traffic jam. Finally, they ditched the car and snatched a motorbike which was suspended on a 45° angle in the middle of a turn.

The trip through the streets was spent in disturbed silence, as each of them stared, disbelieving, at the stone-dead world around them. Neither of them spoke, because neither wanted to consider the implications of this strange situation: either they were insane, or reality was broken. Neither was comforting.

Mirokov lived in a nice upper-middle-class suburb. Kolby had always been jealous of this: he lived in a shitty little apartment downtown. They pulled into the driveway, and when he climbed out of the car, he was amused to see the neighbour mowing the lawn... indefinitely. He laughed bitterly, walked over there, and pulled the guy's pants down. Suddenly, a perplexing question came to mind. He turned and jogged back to the house.

Upon entry, he saw Miro standing in the living room.

"Hey buddy, how is it that you can afford to live in a swanky place like this, when I live in a shitty –" he began, then stopped short as he saw Miro's shoulders were hunched and shaking. This giant of a man was *crying*. A few feet away, in the dining room, Ilya was sitting at the table, working on spelling homework, and Polina, his wife, was standing over her, pointing at a word, her mouth open as if she had been speaking. Ilya was most of the way through the word *"captivating"* – she had so far written *"captivati"*. They were both as still as department store mannequins.

"*I had hoped that they wouldn't be like this...*" Miro whispered. "Of course I knew they *would* be, since everything else seems to be, but, you know, I hoped." Tears rolled silently down his cheeks. "I haven't seen my family in a year, and now here I am, and *they can't see me...*" His voice cracked, faded into silence, and he turned away from the scene.

Kolby felt bad. Even if this was a dream or a magnetism-induced hallucination, he didn't like to see his friend hurt. In actuality, he was forcing himself to come to grips with the fact that he actually might *not* be dreaming. This was too clear, too *real*. His dreams were never this coherently organized. He supposed they really *did* go through a wormhole, or something, and lived to tell about it... although there was nobody to listen. He chewed a thumbnail, and placed his other hand sympathetically on Mirokov's shoulder.

"Maybe you should get some sleep, man. We could go and stay at a hotel if it's too emotionally charged here..."

"*I'M NOT LEAVING THEM!!*" Mirokov screamed, shoving Kolby away, who stumbled and fell through the glass coffee table with a terrific crash. He picked himself up out of the scattered glass shards, cursing the cuts on his arms, hands, and back.

"What the *fuck!!* Okay, man! Jesus! We can stay here. But I *really* think both of us need sleep, so I'm going to the guest bedroom. See you in about ten hours." Kolby walked into the bathroom to tend to his wounds – luckily they didn't need stitches. He couldn't bring himself to be mad at Miro... not in this heartbreaking situation.

...

The next morning, things appeared to be the same with Miro's family, and presumably all of Earthship. Kolby awoke feeling a little sore and totally refreshed, but Mirokov looked like he hadn't slept at all.

"Did you even go to bed?" Kolby asked, as he ambled out of the guest bedroom to find Miro sitting on the couch. He didn't need an answer when he saw an empty, overturned rye bottle on the floor. Miro was hunched over, his elbows on his knees and his head in his hands. Kolby didn't know what to do or say, so he just went into the kitchen to fix himself some breakfast. *I didn't even think he drank liquor!* he thought bemusedly to himself.

He had cereal, and discovered the milk was still good, and wondered how long things had been this way, and if the milk would ever spoil. He checked the expiry date, then, realizing he didn't even know the actual date, he booted up the computer in Miro's study. A moment later, Miro winced at the sound of shattering porcelain. Kolby had dropped his cereal bowl, spraying milk and *Happy-O's* all over the floor.

When Mirokov staggered in to holler "What the hell, man!?" he discovered Kolby wide-eyed, staring at the computer screen, silently beckoning him over. He rubbed his eyes, and after a good half minute of effort, managed to squint enough to focus on the tiny characters in the bottom corner of the screen. Instantly, his eyes widened and he stumbled back, losing his balance and collapsing in a heap against the bookshelf. Paperbacks rained down upon him.

The date displayed on the computer was the same day they had left to bring the shipment to *Omega-2-Alpha*.

"How is that possible?!" Kolby stammered.

"How is *any* of this shit possible?" muttered Mirokov, cynically. He picked himself up off the floor and stomped off to the bathroom.

In a daze, Kolby wandered out of the study and back into the dining room. He sat down next to Ilya and rubbed his temples, sighing heavily. *Things just keep getting weirder and...* He glanced over at the paper Ilya was writing on, looked away, then immediately back again, startled. Beneath the child's small hand was written *"capt"*.

"MIRO!!" he hollered,

"What?!" came the muffled reply.

"How far was Ilya on her word yesterday?"

"*Captivati.*"

"Well, she's... regressing."

"What?!" Miro came up behind them, rubbing his face with a towel. "Well, I'll be buggered! What do you suppose that means?" he exclaimed in genuine stupefaction, forgetting for a moment his hangover and misery.

"Damned if I know."

They checked again four hours later. The solitary letter "*c*" stared up at them. Time was reversing, and it was accelerating. Together they watched in horrified awe, as Ilya's hand crept backwards over the page, slower than the minute hand of a clock, erasing, with the sharpened tip of her pencil, the word she had just written.

...

Two hours hence, the two men stood and gawked as Polina slowly unwashed the dishes. Then, she and the child sat together at the table, carefully reaching into their mouths with their empty forks and pulling out bites of food, placing them in neat little piles on their plates. When they had each assembled a perfect-looking meal in this manner, Polina picked the plates up, walked backwards into the kitchen, and methodically unmade dinner, using a knife to glue the pieces of vegetables back together, then stowing all the ingredients tidily in the refrigerator.

Never at any point had either she or Ilya acknowledged the existence of Miro and Kolby. It was as if they were simply a scripted video running in reverse. Their speech, and all sound, in fact, was also reversed, and stretched out corresponding to the current speed of time reversal. Outside, the neighbour unmowed his lawn, oblivious to his lowered drawers.

Yet another bizarre phenomenon occurred when Polina sat down on the couch to read a magazine while drinking a cup of coffee. When they had arrived, a stack of magazines had been resting on the table; when Kolby plunged through it, shattering the glass, they had scattered all over the floor. However, when Polina sat down, she reached to pick up a magazine, as if it were still there, but her hands were empty. At the same time, she had placed her mug of coffee on the non-existent table, but, instead of falling, it simply hovered in space.

"Apparently, we're putting quite a bit of stress on this reality..." Kolby mused, "We're operating in one temporal framework, manipulating physics accordingly, while the rest of the universe conforms to a completely different, pre-recorded paradigm. If this were a computer program, the most likely response would be a total system malfunction: identical iterations of code are constantly trying to countermand and contravene each other – there would be catastrophic failure of the system." He chewed on a fingernail thoughtfully. "I wonder how it would manifest in the physical universe – some sort of shattering of atomic space and perceptual reality – perhaps an immense detonation of nuclear fission would cause the total destruction of the eternal cosmos, rippling outwards at a phenomenal rate, like another big bang? *Would something new come of it, or would it be the end of everything?*"

...

The two men received quite a shock, when morning arrived backwards, and Mirokov – that of the Earthship reality, that is – came home, or rather, he unleft. In exactly the opposite sequence the real Miro had carried out, he went through the motions of kissing his wife and child hello, unpacking his suitcase, regurgitating his breakfast, performing an extremely disturbing exchange with the toilet, and going to bed. The real Miro was understandably shaken up. Incidentally, the time reversal was still getting faster.

"It's increasing logarithmically," stated Kolby. "Instead of a linear, constant progression, it is increasing on a curve, getting faster and faster with each passing moment. At some point, it will all just be a blur, I imagine."

"And what about us? What about *them?*" asked the distraught Mirokov, gesturing to the bedrooms, where his eerie doppelganger and his family were in repose, but getting less and less sleep by the second.

"Well, we seem to be separate from this time-space continuum. At some point, everything around us will be moving so fast, it will shift to a higher

Earthship : Devolution

vibrational frequency. At this moment we can interact with objects, but soon, we'll probably turn into ghosts. As for them... and everything else, I imagine it will just keep getting younger and younger. Which reminds me, I'd like to go find myself."

Mirokov spoke quietly, his head bowed. "Ezra... I can't leave. My place is here... in whatever form. With my family."

"I don't *have* a family!" snapped Kolby, suddenly irritated. "I live on my own in a tiny apartment in a shit section of town. I don't have a grand home and a wife and kids! At least you have *that* to look back on! You and your well-to-do lifestyle. Christ!!" He turned away angrily. After a moment, Miro's empty-sounding voice resounded from behind him.

"You asked how I could afford this place, since we have equal pay? ... *I can't.* Have a look at my chequebook! Everything is written in red. I was counting on this shipment to help with my debt. Otherwise we were going to have to default on seven charge cards, and the mortgage, and soon thereafter, we'd probably have been on the streets. Due to creditors, I wouldn't even have been able to afford a tiny apartment in a shit section of town. I was *bankrupt*, Ezra. In some sense, what has happened here is a blessing, because now, that will never happen! Now, everything that occurs *is* a certainty, because I've already done it all! At least I won't have to lay awake at night, worrying and trying to drown my fear and anxiety with secret drinking binges, when everyone else is asleep, because I am too damn cowardly to face the reality that my beautiful, innocent little girl might soon be homeless, because I *failed* as a father and provider. And *you?* You may live paycheque to paycheque, but at least you don't owe your entire life to the bank, and credit card companies. At least you don't have dependants to worry about. At least you're *free* in a way a family man will *never* be, no matter how much he loves them."

Mirokov's eyes sparked with rage and bitter anguish. "So yeah... you go and "find yourself". This is my last stop. Remember what I said to you before? "Death is the incontrovertible admission that my loved ones and I will never see *each other* again." Well, the definitive moment has come and gone: *I've been dead since yesterday afternoon.* It's been nice knowing you, pal."

Mirokov stood and embraced his friend before retiring to his bedroom, closing the door with finality, and locking it. Kolby just stood there, speechless, his jaw on the floor, ashamed of his outburst. Through the door, he apologized pathetically, but received silence in response. Feeling the heavy sorrow of great and sudden loss, he shuffled out of the house and began the long walk home.

...

It didn't take too long for Kolby to become bored of watching himself unlive his own life. He'd already been there; it was old news. He walked into the countryside and found a solitary hill where he was fairly certain he

Earthship : Devolution

wouldn't be hit by some backwards-zipping automaton. Now that the streets were bizarrely active, cars were motoring backwards; it was no longer safe to drive, or even walk, for a temporally-forward-oriented individual. He sat beneath a tree, shaded from the hot sun, absently pulling out single blades of grass.

How he had *yearned* to be home, to see the welcoming blue sky and the shimmering glass of Earthship's exterior shell, instead of the cruel, heartless black of space. He had so desired to walk in grass, to smell the forest, to be home again!

Now, he had the absurd realization that he had no home. It wasn't just because of this weird time shit, either – he hadn't had a home even before they had left.

He thought back on Mirokov's sentiments, about how a person could be alive, but still be dead, if they had nobody who loved them. If that's the truth, Kolby had always been dead. He never knew his parents: he grew up in an orphanage among hundreds of other faceless wretches whom it was illegal to put down like dogs. He had no life to speak of before this, and if it weren't for time reversing faster and faster, he could easily have continued living the exact same life with everyone around him as statues. It's not as if they could have noticed him any less. He had never had a girlfriend. All he had was Miro.

I guess that was a kind of love... he mused, but it just felt cheap and pathetic, a long stretch of a desperate man, which was exactly the truth of it, and it pissed him off. Angrily, he tore up handfuls of rich brown soil and luscious green grass, and pounded the dirt with his fists, but when he was done, he didn't feel any better at all.

...

As time sped up ever more rapidly, Kolby discarded his misery, becoming much more interested in seeing the rest of Earthship revert. As he had suspected, he indeed became incorporeal as the molecules of everything around him accelerated to a higher vibrational plane. This was really quite fortunate, because at the speed everything was moving, if he had been hit by something or someone zipping by in reverse, it would have flattened him like a train, killing him instantly.

Instead, he got to watch an epic saga unplay itself. He watched as Earthship was developed, populated, built, and planned. Before it collapsed into nothingness, Kolby witnessed the destruction of Earth. He saw firsthand the effect of nuclear war on such a massive scale the planet became unstable at its core.

Earthship : Devolution

Following the launching of numerous powerful warheads by the UCA (The United Continents of America, having forcefully assumed control of the entire Western hemisphere), he witnessed an explosion so vast it wiped out all of Central and Western Asia, in simultaneous strikes against Turkey, Israel, Syria, Lebanon, Kuwait, Jordan, Iraq, Iran, Afghanistan, The Palestinian Territories, and The United Arab Emirates, leaving a gaping crater 3,853 kilometers in diameter, covering 6% of Earth's circumference.

The planet was actually knocked off its rotational axis, and began to wobble. This drastically affected the weather patterns, producing droughts, famine, earthquakes, floods, hurricanes, tsunamis, and other devastating disasters, and along with them came disease, violence, and more war.

It was the megaton nuclear bomb, fired by a United Korea, which finished the job. A crater covering a further 8% of the globe finally destroyed the despotic UCA, as well as cracking the planet's crust so deeply that new volcanoes formed over the globe, dousing the Earth in seething magma. Pompeii looked like an EZ-Bake Oven in comparison. This was followed by global nuclear winter, radiation sickness, birth defects in the form of horrendous mutations, and the total collapse of civilization.

This had been long foreseen, however, and Earthship had been under construction for two centuries before the first bomb dropped. It was finally completed just before the final warhead fell, and certain choice selections of the remainder of humanity – that is, the parts of Central Europe that were still standing – were transported to the Earthship. The rest of surviving humankind was deemed not valuable enough to save, and, in order to prevent some sort of planetary collision (but mostly just to wipe away the unsightly evidence of the human race's Ultimate Fuck-Up), Earthship launched millions of tons of nuclear explosives in the form of one package the size of Japan, then high-tailed it out of there. When they were far enough away that the Earth appeared as big as its moon had appeared from the planet's surface, the bomb was detonated, and the remains of the once-blue planet, by that point a tomb of red, white, and black, was vaporized in an explosion that rocked Earthship, even at a distance of 2.5 million miles.

Floating in space, impervious to the ultrasound vibrations of the physical universe he was somehow disconnected from, Kolby watched all of this refold with increasing rapidity. He watched further and saw the decolonization of Earth, and the re-emergence of the dinosaurs.

At long last, he saw the continents reform into *Pangaea*, floating as one luscious, green land mass upon a sphere of scintillating blue ocean. It was the most perfect sight he had ever witnessed. He had the certain conviction that if it had remained that way, totally unmarred by humankind, it would have forever been a utopia. Then, beneath his captivated gaze, the Earth disappeared completely, as the universe rapidly shrank in upon itself, ultimately coalescing in a reverse cataclysmic explosion, into one small, glowing, brilliantly white ball of energy.

Ezra Kolby drifted up to it, surrounded by... nothingness. Not even the blackness of space. Just... *nothing.* The sphere was the size of a golf ball. It burned fiercely, and beneath its surface churned a dense collection of protons, neutrons, and electrons, all vibrating with the rage of one hundred octillion suns. Even as Kolby watched, this, too, shrank and winked out, like a snuffed candle flame.

Within this limitless negativity of matter, Kolby looked around him, feeling for all the universe like a person in a dark theater, wherein the film had ended but the lights were never turned back on.

That's it? He thought. *What do I do now??*

Remembering something from Sunday school, so many eons ago *(or was it in the future, now?)*, he shrugged, and said, experimentally:

"Let there be light."

...and there was light.

[2016-06-21/23:39:14]

The Dragon Catcher

On his thirty-third birthday, Jeremias Joakim Sauveterre was turned inside out. This was precipitated by the declassification and subsequent commercialization of the *Telepathic/Telekinetic Physical Matter Transmogrification Device,* otherwise known as the Telefantasy Machine (TFM).

Some explanation is in order.

Quite frankly, mankind has shown itself to be incredibly ingenuitive when it comes to avoiding the dismal or depressing aspects of the human condition. Within the dancing, spiralling smoke of the pipe dreams of earlier centuries, citizens wasted away under the devastation of prolonged abuse of drugs such as opium, cocaine, amphetamines, and their derivatives. Later centuries escaped into the digital age of virtual reality: it was not uncommon for fanatics to be found in full-body stimulation suits, like wetsuits containing millions of tiny electrodes which stimulated nerve endings all over the body, producing hyper-realistic sensations. Fully-isolating helmets provided visual and auditory immersion, while gyroscopic suspension gear allowed users to feel weightless, free of the undeniable, disappointing sensations of sitting in a chair or even standing upon ground, which consistently shattered the illusion of flying, swimming, or other "recreational activities" requiring more dynamic or creative positioning of the body. The gyroscopic gear consisted of a thick ring of titanium, 2m in diameter, within the center of which users were suspended, via four thin, strong metal fibres attached to the hips and shoulders of their immersion suit. This ring of titanium was set within another ring of a slightly larger diameter, which, through several ingeniously-designed sets of bearings, allowed users to pivot, spin, and rotate in any direction, upon all axes, to unlimited degrees, corresponding to whatever they happened to be experiencing within the simulation. The body's own auditory-vestibular system responded to this, creating sensations of altered gravity or orientation.

It became an epidemic. Citizens bound themselves into their immersion rigs for hours, then days, weeks, and months at a time: by hooking their bodies up to IV nutrient drips and waste-diverting catheters and enema tubes, they could ostensibly remain within their virtual reality indefinitely. In reality, however, the human body simply was not designed for such abuse, and it was sadly commonplace for the odours which seeped under a user's apartment door to shift from acrid sweat and leaking waste products, to that of undeniable putrefaction. A toll-free number was dialled, and a cleanup squad would arrive, outfitted in hazardous materials suits and gas masks. A common remark one might have heard within the locker rooms after a day's rounds of "urban environment sanitation", was that, no matter how many times an emergency responder experienced it, he still got a chill down his spine when he prised the isolation helmet off a user, revealing the moist, steaming, bone-white skin, wrinkled and soft like dishpan fingertips, within which sunken, milky eyes peered, wide and staring, ghoulish and ghastly, into the soul of the poor medical personnel, who was, after all, just doing his job. Such was life, however, no different than any other of the gritty realities of the age, such as government-mandated eugenics and euthanasia, for example. If the tooth is rotten, it must be pulled. It was as simple as that.

Virtual reality was closely followed by electrostimulation, or "Jacking On", which forewent all the elaborate equipment in favour of a very small hardware installation into a person's natural wetware: at about a third of the cost, and considerable risk, an underground procedure could be performed which installed a series of female jacks, including a 3.5mm stereo audio jack, and a standard HDMI connector for high-resolution video input. Several dozen microelectrodes were attached to certain areas of the primary auditory and visual cortices. Additional input cables did not carry simulated sensory information as such, but instead fed electrodes to certain areas of the neocortex such as the somatosensory cortices, and subcortical structures such as the mesolimbic dopamine pathway, the amygdala, and the hippocampus. These voltage patterns stimulated these structures to produce chemical neurotransmitters, activating pre-existing patterns of experience with respect to physical touch and sensation, emotion, and memory, among many others. In this way, a user could obtain a full-sensory virtual experience simply by plugging a few cables into his or her skull. It was not uncommon for these users to die of starvation or dehydration: since the procedure fully hijacked the apperceptive system, the users literally had no idea they were hungry or thirsty, even up until the moment they gave up the ghost. And this was assuming the procedure was even successful. Morgues and sanatoriums were full of victims of botched surgeries, which killed them, if they were lucky, or left the subjects alive, their brains totally cross wired and scrambled, if unlucky. This produced highly variable effects which rivalled some of the most vicious known neurological disorders. It was for this reason Jacking On was immediately made illegal, but since when has that stopped anyone?

After centuries rife with global epidemics of initially novel but increasingly common means by which a person could die of escapism, there was a roaring public outcry. Mothers were sick of losing their teenagers, wives their husbands, and so forth... the epidemic affected everybody. Even children as young as eleven had been discovered furtively Jacking On in their bedrooms or bathrooms at home, or even in school. The underground surgeons didn't care who they altered, as long as they paid, which was never an issue for the rich kids who stole their parent's charge cards.

This disease desperately needed to be cured, but how? Now, more than ever, they needed *science*. They needed it to provide them with a means, finally, by which they could stop *chasing the dragon*. They needed a way to safely obtain their greatest desires, once and for all, so they could finally get

The Dragon Catcher

back to living their lives in such a way that they no longer yearned to incontinently flee from their own subjective experience.

Thusly was produced *The Dragon Catcher...* the TFM.

It was a machine simple in appearance. It resembled a portable toilet: merely an isolated booth enclosed on all sides, with a door, and a bench to sit on. A user would provide a hefty fee, and the machine would instantly transmogrify them into whatever form fit their greatest desires. The operators of the machine merely took the cash and made sure the juice was running; the choice was known only to each individual client. Many times, clients would step into the machine without even knowing what they wanted to become, but by reading their thoughts, feelings, and innermost desires, the machine carried it out faultlessly, every time.

Some people were transformed into flying beings. Others were given the power of invisibility. Some were made immensely strong, if they were weak, or beautiful, if they were ugly. Wouldn't there be inevitable backlash within a society which allowed any ordinary citizen to be bestowed with magical powers? Probably. But it was just too lucrative to pass up. Besides, if any of them acted out, they'd be promptly and brutally taken care of by the military police. The people were terrified of them. It was doubtful anyone would cause any trouble; even Superman couldn't withstand the force of a Molecular ReAssignment ray, which, at random, turned every type of atom in the body into some other random element. Carbon might become hydrogen, and upon contact with water and oxygen, the person instantly combusted into flames. Such a terrifying weapon did not invite many uses. Consequently, the officials weren't worried. They had thought of everything.

This was, of course, until Jeremias Joakim Sauveterre stepped up to the cashier's terminal, paid his fees and entered the booth. At that point, everything changed.

...

Jeremias Joakim Sauveterre was an unassuming man who lived an unassuming life. He was of an average height, but skinny, and it was quite typical for those who saw him to have the peculiar certainty that he was extremely breakable. At thirty-two, he was not particularly fragile of body, but he felt it of mind. He wore a brown tweed suit every day, because it was the only one he had. His knobby wrists and ankles protruded from the sleeves and cuffs, much like his ears protruded from the sides of his head. He had bad teeth, a hooked nose, and an overbite which left him without a chin. His eyes had all the remarkability of a deposit of animal feces, and he kept them aimed south most of the time.

Jeremias worked as a stenographer in the Eugenics Division of his local legislative authority. He was responsible for taking down anything and everything said by the lead eugenicist, Dr. Howard, over the course of his professional hours. Most of the calls were pleasant enough: couples wanting to conceive a baby who was beautiful and smart and talented – the usual. But other times were rather unpleasant, such as enforced eugenics *after* birth.

In one archetypal situation of this sort, Dr. Howard walked briskly down a hospital hall, with Jeremias stumbling along behind him, his hands full of his writing machine and several personal items the good Doctor had demanded he carry. The antiseptic smell of hospitals always affected Jeremias quite negatively: with the nose he had, he must have inhaled at least six times anyone else, that smell: the breath of death covered up by the toothpaste of bleach and ammonia.

He positioned himself underneath his stenograph, or, rather, he positioned it on top of his legs as he sat in the uncomfortably small folding chair. He leaned forward, fingers poised, waiting for Dr. Howard to launch off. Aaand there he went. Jeremias' fingers worked apace.

The doctor told the exhausted woman in the bed, and her husband who stood adjacent, that the baby had Down's syndrome, and according to the Eugenics Act of 3203, was immediately tossed in the clean-disposal acid vat (which doesn't give off harmful carcinogens like the old fashioned incinerators). He gave his sincerest condolences for their loss, and turned on his heel to walk crisply out of the door, the tails of his white lab coat fluttering.

Bashfully, Jeremias collected his things and followed, blushing awkwardly upon seeing the looks of shock, exhaustion, and grief which had only now begun to make the gamut of the newly-ex-newly-parents' faces.

...

He found himself forced, every day, twice a day, to take the subway to work and back. He resented every moment crammed into those tin cans speeding rapidly through their dark tunnels like supersonic worms. He could smell each and every passenger on this train, and they were all repugnantly pungent. There was never even enough room to sit down, so he would stand, clutching desperately to an overhead railing, while he felt on all sides the pressure of warm, moist, *unfamiliar* bodies pressing and rubbing against his own, in proximities so intimate he couldn't even bear the thought of doing it with a wife or girlfriend (if only he could earn one), let alone the public transit system. It was utterly humiliating and revolting, and he spent the whole time looking down at his toes, trying to block out the smells, the sounds, and the sensations.

...

When he heard about the *Telepathic/Telekinetic Physical Matter Transmogrification Device*, Jeremias was ecstatic. It was exactly what he needed! But the fee was abominable, so for three years, he pinched his

The Dragon Catcher

pennies, until he had finally saved up enough crumpled, filthy bills and patinated coins to afford a *"TeleFantasy Transmogrification".*

The nearest TFM to him was a two hour long subway ride beneath the urban slums of the metropolis he called home. He felt like a grotto-dwelling troll, grotesque and bent, climbing from the dark, stifling underground into the open air, but the state of affairs wasn't much different at the superterranean level. A thick, almost solid layer of smog hung threateningly only meters above his head, as if the sky really had fallen. The streets were littered with trash, drug paraphernalia, pornographic magazines, alcohol bottles, puddles of vomit in various stages of evaporation, and scores of filthy vagrants milling about, fighting and bickering, and whatever else it was they did.

Jeremias picked his way along the sidewalk, trodding upon tenacious weeds clinging to life within the cracked concrete and shattered glass. Eventually, he got to the TFM center, only to find that the lineup was longer than the subway ride, and just as noisy, smelly, and cramped.

When he finally got to the front of the line, he had a vicious headache; it felt like his skull was being split down the middle. His name was requested; he replied that he was Jeremias Joakim Sauveterre. Then, he was told to read and sign a waiver, and a payment invoice. He signed both documents without looking, handed the man an envelope of cash, and waited in embarrassment as the ticketer was forced to count it all, griping audibly the whole time. At long last, everything was in order, and he was ushered into the booth. The walls were painted a grubby off-white shade, and the stool was round and set to one side of the booth, whereas on the other side was a full-length mirror. The operator closed the door.

Abruptly, everything went black, but soon, Jeremias could see two blue lights before him, and in the mirror saw two more behind; they had begun blinking in all four upper corners of the booth. As they moved closer with a distinctly robotic noise, a single light bulb switched on directly above him, giving him the impression of being isolated in a tiny circle of light amidst endless blackness.

The blue lights belonged to autonomic arms, which extended probes towards his head from all sides. Jeremias crushed his eyes shut, and wrung his trembling hands, his rising excitement cresting its apogee.

*This is **IT!!***

...

Outside the TFM, the booth rumbled and hummed contentedly, as usual, and this noise was overlaid by the derisive comments of two of the staff, who were betting whether Jeremias would come out a model, a bodybuilder, or a professional wrestler, considering how God-damned ugly he was.

Presently, the machine stopped, and the handlers waited for the door to burst open and vomit forth whatever ludicrous creation would end up parading before them. But no such thing occurred. So, the handlers opened the door themselves. What they saw inside made them turn their heads and gag. It was Jeremias Joakim Sauveterre, or something that used to be him.

Sitting upon the bench was a bizarre display of human internal anatomy. Jeremias had literally been turned inside out, as one might expect to happen if they shoved a bunch of entrails into a glove, then inverted it. His intestines were all over the floor, his stomach hanging there, a slippery purple sack. His liver and kidneys were clearly visible, also. All of the muscle tissue remained, but it was oriented outwards, still holding onto the bones, which were now resting indolently upon the mess, as if their function had outlived their form.

The rib cage had been completely bent back, along the axis of the spine, so that (looking from the top or bottom) what had originally been $\mho$-shaped, now appeared as a ω-shape. Traversing the body 360° revealed muscle layer all around, indicating that the skin was now on the inside, oriented towards the center.

The most astounding discovery of the whole grisly spectacle was that Jeremias Joakim Sauveterre was still *ALIVE*. His heart, hanging off the front of this pile of viscera, remained pumping. All his organs were quivering and pulsating with life, as if nothing unusual had happened.

Even his skull had been somehow turned inside out: the sharp, jagged edges of the inside of the plates were clearly visible. The brain was hanging from the brainstem, but backwards – where the face ought to have been. The eyes could be seen as optic nerves extending into the inverted skull. The medics on site marvelled at this: if Jeremias were sensate, and not in horrible agony, could he see *into* himself? Certainly not, it would be pitch black. At the best, he might be able to perceive a diffuse red, due to leakage of light through the optic nerves and retinas.

One thing was clear: Jeremias could certainly not communicate, and there was no coming back from *this*. They concluded there must have been a malfunction of the transmogrification system. Poor, unfortunate bastard. The doctor decided the most humane thing to do would be to swiftly put him out of his misery. After a discussion with her colleagues, and the CEO of the company, who had teleported there as soon as he heard the outrageous news, they agreed that Jeremias should be euthanized. The doctor readied a syringe, the contents of which she intended to inject straight into the heart. She quietly approached the mangled remains of Jeremias Joakim Sauveterre, and whispered her respects to the tragic end of the young man, crossing her heart in a silent rosary. She slowly guided the tip of the needle, glistening with a single drop of sodium pentobarbital, towards that purple, convulsing heart.

When the point of the needle was a hair's breadth away from the tissue, another fantastic thing happened: the doctor quite unexpectedly compressed into a wet, bloody ball of meat, bone, hair, and fabric, the size of a soccer ball. It hung bizarrely in the air for a few microseconds before dropping, impacting the white tile floor with a gruesome *splat*, spraying jagged shard patterns of blood in an outward radius.

Panicking and cursing, the TFM controllers and the other medical professionals scrambled over each other in their attempt to immediately be nowhere near whatever was responsible for the nightmarish grotesquery which lay in a warm pile before them.

The CEO stood unmoving, however. He was irritable. First the machine had malfunctioned, horribly mutilating a client, then *this* had happened… whatever it was. It would be a total PR mess. He would be sued into the ground, maybe even indicted on criminal charges. Even worse, he knew that once this got out, sales would plummet, and his tidy profit would become a formidable deficit.

The CEO wearily rubbed a hand across his face, before turning to find a caffeine dispensary.

…

Jeremias Joakim Sauveterre crushed his eyes shut, and wrung his trembling hands, his rising excitement cresting its apogee.

*This is **IT!!***

The probes reached out and clamped onto his head. He heard a faint humming sound, then a brief crepitation of electricity. A shining needle reached out from somewhere and he felt a cold sensation as it bit into his throat and injected some sort of venom into a carotid artery, which made him dizzy and blurred his vision. His heart began to pump so rapidly it hurt. His mind was racing; he felt as if he had no control over his own internal universe. It was as if a hand had entered his brain and was thumbing through the files there. Desultory snippets of his life flashed through his mind, like the scenery past a locomotive's window. He saw himself at six years old, eating an ice cream cone and laughing. Then he found himself at his high school prom, standing alone in the corner, surrounded by hundreds of beautiful young couples devouring each other in love or lust or whatever it was that sparked between the eyes of those dancing young fools, as they celebrated their forsaken childhood, ignorant to the harsh realities which lay ahead.

They drifted in this timeless limbo, where everything was possible because it was all just a game and they were invincible.

Except for Jeremias. He just sat, alone, and stared. He watched each couple, pretending he *was* that boy, and she was *his* girl. Each pair was a different life, in an alternate reality. What might have been, if he were not himself. What was it like to be them? To have each other? And, why were there so many fulfilled and joyful people parading before him, when he was sitting alone? It seemed unfair.

When he couldn't stand it anymore, he walked most of the way home before passing out in a muddy ditch under the persuasion of the bottle of gin he had been hitting hard the whole way. He had felt a profound bitterness, a stomach-turning antipathy for the people all around him, within which he had never belonged.

This memory was just one of many that cruelly invaded his brain, unexpected and unwanted. Jeremias wished it to stop. He had changed his mind, he wanted to get out of this booth of nightmares and go home to bed. But it didn't stop. It got worse.

Abruptly, he felt a sharp pain in his wrists. He looked down, astonished and horrified to find small incisions which were rapidly deepening and quickly lengthening up his forearms and over his biceps. Their source was befuddlingly absent. Was he hallucinating? Back at the wrists, the incisions also traveled in the opposite direction, branching, until each finger was sliced to the bone, lengthwise. He flexed his arm and wiggled his fingers experimentally. He could see the muscles and nerve fibres within the blood which pooled in shimmering rivers, then overflowed down his arms. The pain was enough to make him gag; he experienced hot flashes and reeled in vertigo, but he found he couldn't make a single sound. He could only watch as the same incisions bisected his feet, toes, and legs, before ascending silently up his torso in one final slice which easily cleaved his abdominal muscles and breastplate. He could see his intestines about to spill out, but then the incision was at his chin, his mouth, his nose, his lips, between his eyes! He was overwhelmed with panic and was hyperventilating; he couldn't come to grips with meeting death.

But before he had time to even try, he felt an enormous pressure from an outside source, slowly, agonizingly peeling his body apart. He felt his skull split, and his eyes begin to diverge. He fainted from the searing pain.

...

When Jeremias Joakim Sauveterre awoke, he knew he must be dead. No one could survive such horrors. Furthermore, he felt nothing. No pain, no sensation of any sort. Yes, he *must* be dead! Yet, he had the eerie sensation that his eyes were closed, which was so disturbing because of the inexplicable assurance with which he *knew* he had no eyes to close. Slowly, he willed himself to open his – to receive visual input within his consciousness.

The Dragon Catcher

Stars. He saw stars. What had happened? Perhaps the procedure went horribly wrong, so they thought him dead and tossed him outside, and now night had fallen and he was lying on his back on the lawn. He looked down, only to discover he had no body. All he could see were more stars.

This consciousness called himself Sauveterre, for he was not Jeremias anymore; he was something *bigger*. No longer did he feel the confinement of his inadequate, ugly body. He did not feel fear, insecurity, or loneliness. He felt expansive and eternal. He felt Godlike. The petty gripes and sorrows of his past life seemed trivial and childish, in this new form. He even found he could barely remember it, like one struggles to recall a dream upon awakening, which had been so vivid and perhaps terrifying, yet now is merely a ghost fading into the darkness of the subconscious.

The inky blackness of space extended in all directions to infinite. He could see billions of stars with perfect clarity. He saw galaxies and constellations and solar systems of all sorts, some like monolithic saw blades, swirling circular discs with jagged edges. Others looked like softly drifting cirrus clouds, heading someplace in no particular hurry. And the *colours*. Many of these galaxies had the appearance of paint on a palette, which has had a tool dragged through it in swirls and patterns, intermixing and creating rainbows of swirls, spirals, and whorls. These entire galaxies shimmered and gleamed with luminescent hues of every range. It was surely beautiful.

Sauveterre decided he very much wanted to see this up close. With a mere thought, he found himself instantaneously in the middle of one of these galaxies. It was littered with what must have been planetary debris, but these were no ordinary asteroids. Each one of them reflected a full spectrum of light and colour in its polished silver surface. Sauveterre was in awe.

He skimmed through countless galaxies and solar systems. He approached a giant blue star, its edges blinding tongues of white flame constantly shifting, morphing, and reaching out into the adjacent blackness. The surface of the star was a deep sapphire blue with whorls of topaz, like a globe of pure azurite. Upon its surface, white clouds of hydrogen gas swirled and churned violently, winds strong enough to rip to atoms the entire earth, instantly.

He witnessed a star collapsing into a dense core, then exploding in a devastating supernova which sent waves of energy and elemental material blasting outwards at trillions of kilometers a second. These elements would create new nebulas and new worlds! After the detonation, all that remained was a small neutron star, its surface a restlessly shifting mass of deep orange and black. It was so dense, even a teaspoon of neutron matter would weigh hundreds of millions of tons.

Sauveterre witnessed myriad levels of life. Some were merely protoplasmic, others were sentient creatures with ways he might have considered barbaric, others were highly developed civilizations. This tour of easily sauntering trillions of light years between cosmic destinations and exploring their variegated creatures and cultures, seemed to occupy months, but in the same time, Sauveterre was certain that no time at all had passed. In fact, he was certain whatever he had become was *out-of-time*. Yes, certainly he was dead and was an angel, or a spirit, or something.

Well, if that was the case, Sauveterre decided he wanted to go pay a visit to Jeremias' body, to see what had ended up killing him like this. In the blink of an eye he had located the Milky Way, and his solar system, zooming in on Earth to the exact coordinates where he had last remembered being alive. It was if he were somehow drawn to that particular location by some innate gravitational force; he could feel it *pulling* his consciousness more strongly the closer he came.

Upon reaching the TFM building, he immediately found that he was invisible to people, and that he could fly through walls, which conformed to his postulate regarding his premature expiration. He quickly located the particular booth room he had been in. Instead of the throngs of lines he had been caught up in upon arrival, now the place was practically deserted. Perhaps it was after business hours? He peered at the wall clock, and was astonished to see that less than four minutes had passed since he had stepped into the TeleFantasy Machine.

He could hear the controllers and the medical personnel all arguing together. There had been some disastrous malfunction. They were going to euthanize the client. *Jeremias? Me?* Sauveterre thought, realizing that if he were soon to be euthanized, he couldn't possibly be dead. He was about to go look inside the booth, when he noticed a curious phenomenon. Standing a ways away from the others, the CEO of the company was sitting, griping to himself, but the exceptional thing is that his lips weren't moving. Rather, Sauveterre discovered he could hear every thought in the man's head. He could even *feel* the man's emotions. He had a dizzying sense of omniscience.

Leaving the CEO to his mutterings, Sauveterre glided over to the TFM pod, and looked inside. He observed with detached indifference the ghastly state of Jeremias' body, then attempted to look into *his* mind. He saw himself, looking into himself, looking into himself, looking into himself, on and on, into an infinite regression. He pulled back, reeling with vertigo, then closely examined Jeremias' body. It was true: his heart was pumping, his lungs were pulsating, his intestines were constricting – everything seemed to be working just fine... albeit on the wrong side of the skin. He mused about this.

His new mind worked incredibly quickly, and seemed to have absolutely every datum of information ever conceived by mankind stored in his memory. He had become some sort of a bodiless, ghostly supercomputer. Within a few nanoseconds, Sauveterre divined this:

The human body is nothing more than a vast collection of cells and nuclei, composed of innumerable configurations of electrons, protons, and neutrons.

The Dragon Catcher

All we are is interactions of physics and chemistry, layered upon each other. Without the soul, this is the extent of us; it is all we are. The soul is the infinitely powerful cosmic entity which gives us true life. It has enough power and volition to animate what is essentially dead matter. Even if the body is alive, but lacks a soul, we are merely catatonic – the engine is running but there is no driver.

Yet what about nonhuman animals, which get along just fine without a soul?

Animals don't have a soul as such; rather, they have a more primal version of the powerful divine entity which controls them: the instinct. Humans are much more sophisticated in what their souls can accomplish. The Bible states that God made Man out of His own image. Over centuries and millennia, humans have misconstrued this meaning to believe that God was an upright bipedal primate – that the image of Him is that which we portray with our physical bodies. No, the image of Himself that God imprinted upon humans is that of the eternal, cosmic soul.

So, why are we not all omnipotent?

We are trapped within our bodies. The soul has the ability to animate our bodies, and a great deal more, but is confined within this mortal shroud. When Jeremias was turned inside out, his soul was turned outside in, and was thusly released into the universe. This is the consciousness which identifies as Sauveterre, and since the soul is not matter, it takes up no definable point in space: therefore, it takes up every point in space. It is omnipresent, because it is not confined to the constraints of the physical world. Now, the soul that is Sauveterre is free to use its power to affect whatever it touches, which, of course, is everything. To put it mildly, Sauveterre had become akin to God.

But if that is the case, shouldn't we all become God when we die, and our soul is released from our body?

A soul is non-physical; a body is physical. In order for a soul to exercise volition over the physical world, it needs to be tied to the physical world by way of the body, otherwise it is just an incorporeal ghost or spirit.

Therefore, in order for Sauveterre to exist, he must protect his body **at all costs!**

He reasoned all this within the time it takes to blink, then he saw the doctor, syringe in hand, extending the needlepoint to the flesh of Jeremias' beating heart. Overcome with passion, he channelled his cosmic power, reaching out with it as if he willed the very energy around him to become his body.

Abruptly, the doctor was crushed into a warm, wet, perfectly spherical ball of meat, bone, hair, and fabric, which impacted the floor with a revolting *splat*. Sauveterre gazed raptly upon the product of his actions. He hadn't meant to kill the lady, but it got the job done.

He looked up at the body of Jeremias, volatile and prone to infection or laceration. Every care must be taken to protect that body! He would use every power available to him to ensure it was done! Experimentally, he focused on the mind of the CEO who had just turned to leave for coffee. Abruptly, the man stopped. A strange expression passed over his face, like the reflection of a wax museum lineup in dark glass. He immediately changed direction, raising his hand imperiously and calling for several employees to make arrangements for Jeremias' body to be shipped to a secure, top-of-the-line medical facility.

If Sauveterre could have smiled, he would have. As he slowly drifted through the building, taking in the goings-on, he overheard the question of a young lady standing in line for one of the other Telefantasy booths. She asked the person she was with (her sister, Sauveterre knew instantly) what her greatest desire was, which she would manifest within the Dragon Catcher.

Sauveterre thought back to a lifetime ago, and remembered Jeremias' greatest desire. He had wanted to escape the world of people. He had wanted to turn inwards and disappear inside himself. Sauveterre grinned inwardly. There hadn't been any mechanical malfunction whatsoever. The procedure had worked flawlessly.

[2016-06-16 / 12:04:05]

Shrink Your Dead!

It has been a good day for Harvey Wienberg. He has recently become his own boss, so he can work alone, at the hours of his choice. He is a tailor, crafting fine garments for those who desire to advertise their evident stylishness. Of course, Harvey isn't like some of the other tailors in the city – the type who believe newest is best, and quickly adulterate their profession with recourse to machines and computers which do all the measuring and cutting and sewing automatically. Those guys can't even call themselves tailors, Harvey thinks. At best, *Fashion Designer*.

No, there is something quite different about Harvey Wienberg, but it is a very small thing. Harvey lives entrenched in tradition. He was steeped in it from an early age, learning the craft of the needle and tape from his grandfather. Since he was an infant, Harv grew up under the wing of his Pappi and Mammi, after the plane carrying his mother and father decided to rather unproductively plummet from the stratosphere to the soft earth below.

Pappi taught him how to be a real tailor, forsaking automation and digitization, performing with his own two hands, the drawing, measuring, cutting, and stitching, to produce a product he could be proud of. Mammi taught him how to keep a clean and happy home, and his place in the hierarchy of the family. Both taught him class and confidence, to be firmly yourself at your best, no matter what your position in life may be.

Respect authority. Respect authority. Respect authority.

...

From a surreally green front lawn, Harvey admires his modest little bungalow. It's not much, but it's home. He enters and closes the door quietly behind him, then meticulously hangs his hat and coat in the closet, tucking his shoes neatly beneath them.

"Honey, I'm home!" he calls out, as he always does every day, when he returns from work. He absent-mindedly fiddles with the watch on his wrist. A moment later an exuberantly cheerful female voice resounds from the neighboring room.

"*Welcome* home, dear! How *are* you today?"

"Oh, pretty good, Shannon. Got six new clients today. Business is booming!"

He walks into the kitchen, where a tall, slender woman stands with her back to him. She is robed in a loose satin blouse and a flowing dress with lace on the bottom. She wears high heels, and is decorated from tip to toe with baubles and trinkets. Her bleached blonde hair is immaculately styled, in a tall, round, shoulder-length bouffant, perfectly flipped up at the ends. She is heavily made up, with blue eyeshadow and dark red lipstick. She stands motionless, with her hands in a sinkful of dishes. Seeing her there, full-figured and voluptuous, Harvey's fingers flicker neurotically over the face of his wristwatch. Without turning her head, she speaks,

"Your dinner is ready, my darling; it just needs to be heated up!"

"What a peach you are," replies Harv, patting the woman's admirable buttocks and kissing her softly on the cheek. "You've likely been at this all day, your legs must be very sore; why don't you let me take over?" He helps his wife into the living room and into a soft chair, where he drapes a blanket across her. "Thank you, my precious husband!" she hollers exuberantly, as he walks back into the kitchen to finish the dishes and warm up his supper.

Now, where are those kids?

Drying his hands on a towel, Harvey walks into the playroom to find, just as he had expected, his nine year old son and four year old daughter on the floor in front of the television. Billy is sitting cross-legged, while Sally is lying on her tummy, her feet in the air.

"Come on, you two, it's time for supper!" They remain motionless, quietly affixed to the television screen.

"Always a struggle with you kids, isn't it? I should get rid of that television!" Harvey raises his voice, his fingers tapping his watch angrily – but it's just an act, of course. Lately, he has found it impossible to remain angry at them for more than a moment.

After a second's pause, they shout "No, no, please don't!" but remain completely still, staring forward. Harvey sighs with affectionate resignation. *Kids will be kids!* He physically picks up each one of them and carries them into the kitchen, plopping them down in their chairs, and there they sit, silently pouting.

Harvey sets his plate of food in front of him, and a plate in front of each of the children, and sits down to eat. After a few minutes of silence, he speaks:

"So, Billy, how did your baseball game go today?"

After a pause: "Yes Daddy all my homework is done."

"Um", says Harvey, fiddling with his watch, "That's good, son, but how was your baseball game?"

Still staring at the blank wall in front of him, the boy responds. "It was really good! I got a home run and I caught out Johnny Matheson in the second inning!"

"How wonderful! Just like last week! You're really showing improvement; you see, practice makes perfect!"

"Yes, daddy."

Shrink Your Dead!

"Sally, how was your ballet practice?" The little girl is bent forward, with her nose to the plate, apparently inspecting something with great intensity.

"Oh for God's sake, young lady, sit up! Maintain proper posture; how many times have I told you two!" Harvey stands up and roughly straightens the girl's spine. "Like that! Remember: *A sagging spine sums a sad Sally!*"

"Yes, Daddy." says Sally, sitting still and erect. "My ballet practice was very good, Daddy – I learned to pirouette!"

"Tremendous!" Harvey cries out, smiling broadly, and can't help but think to himself:

Life is good!

...

Things weren't always so wonderful, however. Even as recently as one year ago, it was the exact opposite. His kids were disrespectful little punks who would run screaming around the house, obstinately refusing to bow to any authority. Billy tortured his little sister with water pistols, spitball shooters, and pellet guns, and Sally retaliated by screaming at the top of her lungs, then running into his room and wrecking stuff.

It was a fucking madhouse.

Shannon wasn't much help. Soon after Sally was born she fell into post-partum depression, and her latent social anxiety blossomed into robust agoraphobia. She then became addicted to tranquilizers, which she stated were meant to calm her down and help her sleep. They did a wonderful job! When she wasn't sleeping, she was staring serenely at the wall or the television in an oblivious stupor, while two little Tasmanian devils tornadoed around her, sucking everything not bolted down into their vortex of destruction.

Every night, Harvey returned home, stressed about his boss, irritated at his coworkers, and would walk through the door, straight into a war zone. He found food splattered on the ceiling, ghastly murals painted all over the walls, and craft paper, pencil crayons, and toys *everywhere*. The floor could not even be seen.

Frequently, he took his shoes off and stepped directly on the smallest piece of Lego ever manufactured, cleverly designed to be the *most* painful. Or there was the time he put his bare foot down and felt something cold and squishy arise between his toes. He gingerly lifted his foot and looked down. A pair of panties... loaded with the feces of a four year old girl, who apparently hadn't thought it prudent to go to the toilet before *or* after her "accident" and had merely dropped her drawers where she stood. Agape and enraged, Harvey walked into the living room, from where the cacophony resounded the loudest.

Sure enough, there she was, running around the chesterfield, clothed in nothing more than lacey socks and a highly-stained bright yellow shirt that didn't even cover her belly button. Her bum and legs were poopy and she was dragging a large kite behind her, shouting "*Fly, fly, fly away!*" as the obstinate thing clamoured off the walls and floor, in the process clearing every horizontal or vertical surface of anything which had happened to be on it. It also often bounced off Shannon, who was intensely absorbed in a commercial on the family-life-stabilizing power of Sal Hepatica laxative. A jingle chimed merrily.

Hey Pal, take Sal, Sal Hepatica!

Harvey turned on his heel and walked straight back the way he had entered, and over to his friend Jeff's house.

Jeff Malcolm was a taxidermist. He was in his garage working on an owl when he noticed Harvey walk up the driveway.

"What's happening, Harv? Driven out of your own house again by Thing 1 and Thing 2?"

"Can't be. Mother is home. ...Physically, at least." Harvey sat down on an old, worn out office chair. "How's business?"

"Oh, can't complain. Did Mr. Henderson yesterday."

"Mr. Henderson, eh? I was wondering when he'd kick the bucket."

"Yup, and Mrs. Henderson paid fully upfront for his package, *plus* her own. She says it won't be long now till she joins him, and she wants to look her best for her daughter's mantelpiece."

"Gotta love astute consumers. What are you working on there? I thought animal taxidermy had gone the way of the dodo."

Jeff grunted as he popped a glass eyeball into the socket of the dead Great Horned Owl he was working on. "If the dodo is on exhibition in the city's richest private estates, yes, you would be correct. This is the last Great Horned Owl ever in existence, at least that's what the guy told me. Said he was proud to have personally made a species go extinct, and he wants to show everybody his index finger, which, according to him, has "enough power to destroy the culmination of billions of years of evolution, with just a little squeeze.""

Harvey shrugged ambivalently. "Well, whatever." He looked around at the equipment adorning the walls and shelves. While most men his age might have a garage filled with power tools and wood cast-offs, Jeff's walls displayed a wide array of surgical scalpels, electric bone saws, knives, clamps, PVC tubing, and steel hooks. It looked like something out of a low-budget horror movie.

"Hey, where do you keep all your human projects?" Harvey asked.

Shrink Your Dead!

Jeff's face unequivocally expressed the opinion that Harvey was a little bit stupid. "Obviously not in my garage, Harv. Back at the lab. The taxidermy is just one in a production line of events from death to minification. I'm first, then it goes onto the Engineers who machine and install the moving parts, then the Techwizards install the computer hardware and software. After that, the body moves forward to Styling, where its hair and makeup are permanently configured. Finally, when everything has been okayed by the next of kin, miniaturization happens, then onwards to the Tailor to have their last wardrobe assembled. Honestly, the tailors we have aren't very good. I wish I had your skills at my disposal."

"Wait, they're tailoring a tiny wardrobe? Why not just dress the cadavers beforehand?"

"We've had issues miniaturizing people in their clothes: they don't seem to shrink at the same rate. So, we've found it just works better to shrink the person in the nude, and make the clothes for them afterwards. Usually we're working to recreate a life-sized dress or suit they already own. The client thinks the outfit has been miniaturized just like that."

"Hmm. So this whole assembly line... then a little minified human action figure." Harvey mused. "Still blows me away when I think of it."

...

In the year 1350, at the end of the Black Death and Great Famine, the world population of 370 million began growing exponentially, especially after the industrial revolution of 1820. In 2011 the global population had hit 7 billion, and by the year 2729, another 164 billion souls later, real estate area had become a critical commodity. Lakes were drained, swamps filled in, rainforests paved over. Every available square mile was necessarily developed to house the multitudes of filthy humans scuttling along the Earth's crust, scurrying over and around each other like soft cockroaches. All land was devoted to either housing projects or agriculture, with a strictly regulated allowance for commercial space.

One innocent victim of this restructuring was the Undertaker. Graves were considered a waste of valuable space, and fundamentally disrespectful. Why suffocate your dead relative under a ton of earth and let them rot to nothing in the cold, damp, darkness? *How rude!* You will only come to see them maybe twice a year, to stand on top of a slab of concrete and put fresh flowers beside the shriveled or liquefied ones from last year. You will then think, *'Here I am,'* and then not much else other than a sense of futility, and, as soon as you can overcome your guilt, you will hurry away. *Just shameful!*

Instead, why not keep your loved ones in your home with you always, right on the mantelpiece? No, not cremation; that is nearly as rude as neglected putrefaction. Why not have them stuffed! Certainly, the idea seems absurdly impractical: erecting your dead auntie or grandma in the living room, taking up valuable bed space. However, a new solution has arisen.

Shrink Your Dead!!

Here at **Minification Unlimited**, we can turn your loved ones into little seven-inch-tall dolls, resplendent in their Sunday best! Afraid of your favourite uncle getting dusty on a shelf? He *was* the adventurous sort, after all. Have no fear: For a small charge, we can install moving joints, and your minified uncle becomes a stalwart action figure which will entertain your children for hours! (You might even admit that old Uncle Horatio is even more useful now than he was before he passed on.)

Lonely? Miss your wife or husband after that freak portapotty incident that stole them away from you? Install a communication device into their body! **Minification Unlimited** can program into them an unlimited number of audio phrases, either recorded before their death, or chosen from our millions of soundbytes produced by our most skilled voice acting talent, then digitally transmogrified to sound exactly like your loved ones. You won't even know the difference! With a few quick keypresses of the activator, you can have an almost-real conversation with your dead family and friends, as if they were never gone!

So, please, do yourself and your dearly beloved a favour – visit **Minification Unlimited** today, before the opportunity is lost forever!!

...

"But there's one thing I just don't get," said Harvey, speaking carelessly through his corn dog, chunks and crumbs flying from his lips, "If we have developed the technology to shrink people, why isn't this being exploited to its maximum potential? I mean, we've barely got room to breathe here. Maybe they could just pick everyone below a certain socioeconomic level, who are probably responsible for most of the baby-making that's been going on – haven't they heard of birth control?? – and shrink the whole kit and caboodle. The Wife & Kids along with Fluffy the cat and Rex the dog – every one of those little fuckers! We could free up maybe 80% of the space on Earth that way! We wouldn't be killin' anyone, just makin' em real small and less of a pestilence. Then they can fornicate all they like and they'd just produce ugly little microbabies. Hahahaha!!!" Harv took a long pull off his third beer as he thoroughly enjoyed his own joke.

"I'm sure that has been HEAVILY considered." replied Jeff. "Unfortunately, the shrinking process has proven lethal on living subjects. It has to do with the dynamics of molecular size. I'll have you know, I'm not just a taxidermist; I've been in such close quarters with this whole process, I'm practically an expert – I can even run the whole assembly in a pinch.

Shrink Your Dead!

"The process works well for inanimate tissue. But living tissue has an unfortunate side effect. Living bodies are incredibly complex, and a very delicate balance must be observed, in order to maintain the homeostatic equilibrium that life requires. When we go about jiggling the molecules of living things, their natural thermodynamic and kinetic energy increases exponentially, and they literally explode. It's really quite messy – I've seen it." Jeff made a wry face as he gently and carefully preened the owl's feathers.

"And there have been no advancements in technology?" Harvey furrowed his brow and scratched his chin.

"Nothing... definitive. Beyond that I'm obliged to silence. Just know that we've found nothing that is in any way safe or consistently replicable." Jeff's eyes and tone of voice pleaded with his friend to leave it alone and move on. Harvey nodded, and hoisted himself to his feet.

"Well, it was good seeing you, old friend. It's time to go lock the demons in their room so I can change Shannon's diaper in relative peace."

"Good luck, Harv."

...

At home, Harvey Wienberg shut himself up in his room for his "man time". Not that he had any other time, considering that the lives of Shannon and the kids never once coincided with his. They merely bounced or slouched around him.

He turned on the television. After only a few minutes, he began fidgeting in irritation. *Always more of the same shit.*

Since minification was introduced around four centuries ago, lots of cool things have come from it, such as people who have six generations of family set up on their mantelpiece. Some of them are arranged in dramatic tableaus, mimicking popular movies of the time, or historical battles. Some people end up accumulating pretty huge collections of "Minis" over the years, since it isn't uncommon for the less sentimental of them to buy and trade each other's ancestors.

– Your Grampa Joe and his awesome handlebar moustache would look great in the post-apocalypse stop-motion film I'm making. If you give him to me, I'll let you have my little sister.

– She's the little redhead, right? Died of leukemia when she was six?

– Yeah, and she'd make a great addition to the orphanage in your 15th century London arrangement.

– Hmm, yeah, if I get a her a tattered dress and grind her in the dirt a bit, she'd be perfect! Okay, deal!

And so on.

Shrink Your Dead!

Minified celebrities have become a major collector's item, too. After a celebrity dies, a bidding war rivalling Wall St ensues. Unfortunately, this lowers the chances of obtaining a *CelebMini* to next to nil, so the more industrious and morally destitute individuals are often featured on the news as having unsuccessfully attempted to abscond with a celebrity with the intent to prematurely minify them.

What never appears on the news, however, is the disturbingly frequent occurrence of some celebrity or other actually going missing, and subsequently turning up on eBay as a "rare collector's item" CelebMini. When police investigate, flippant denial and the inevitable total lack of evidence muddy the already opaque waters of justice to the point where original ownership or timeline is never discovered, and the matter goes unresolved.

Even worse is the increasing incidence of human trafficking. Refugees from the poorest, most war-torn, disease-ridden, overcrowded locales on Earth: Syria, India, Africa, etc, these totally desperate people are promised a new life. They are told they will be "live-minified", which will allow more of their friends and family to fit on a transport vehicle undetected, with more food to go around, and they will go to America or some other False Promised Land, where they will be enlarged (which is currently impossible, even on inanimate objects).

These impoverished, uneducated people have no idea of the scientific limitations of the technology, so they pay their exorbitant premium and face one of two fates: 1: They are blown apart at a molecular level, in a bloody spray, by some wannabe scientist who thinks he knows what he's doing, or 2: They will arrive, safe and sound, at their chosen destination, packaged in an orderly fashion in cardboard boxes, having been efficiently murdered and minified. They will be sold in bulk to the highest bidder: perhaps some amateur filmmaker, or some-whack-job with a supply of homemade cherry bombs, or some other obsessed pervert.

All of this sickened Harvey. He turned off the television, arose, and stood in front of the door, mentally preparing to brave the bedlam just beyond.

…

"You were amazing, dear!" cooes Shannon Wienberg, after an admittedly one-sided bout of furtive fornication. She lays on her back, completely subdued and motionless, beside a panting, sweaty Harvey Wienberg,

"I… I was, wasn't I? Yeah… You know, you never used to say that to me." He fiddles with the watch on his wrist.

"You were amazing, dear!"

"I bet you tell all the guys that."

"You were amazing, dear!"

"Okay, okay. Now you're descending into empty flattery. I get it! And don't you ever forget it." Harvey sits up in bed and swings his feet over to the floor. He gets up and dons his housecoat before walking into the kitchen for a glass of vitamin water. At the kids' room he pauses, and opens the door. He can see in the semi-darkness both children lying still and silent. He smiles, tiptoes in, and tenderly kisses each of their foreheads, before turning to leave, gently playing with his watch with a finger.

"Daddy, is that you?" Harv stops, his hand on the door handle.

"Yes, honey, it's me. What's up?"

"I can't sleep," states Sally, "Can you read me a story?"

"Well how about I *tell* you a story instead? So we don't wake your brother by turning on the light." He sits on the edge of her bed and lovingly caresses her skin. "You're so cold! Here, bundle up in another blanket."

"Okay, Daddy."

Harv beams with joy. "*Once upon a time, there was a beautiful little princess named Sally...*"

...

"They've done it, haven't they?"

"*Huh?*" Startled, Jeff Malcolm looked up from the marmot carcass he was currently eviscerating. "Who's they? Done what? For God's sake, man, don't sneak up on me like that."

"Live human minification. They – you – have figured it out, haven't you? You're just not allowed to talk about it because of your NDA...?"

"Fuck, Harv!" Agitated, Jeff threw his hands up, flinging soft, wet rodent intestine, which stuck to the ceiling. "I—I told you – "

"Yeah, I know you did. You told me that there was nothing *safe* or *consistently replicable* or *definitive*. But this means that you *do* have something!! Right? Look, I know you can't answer that, but answer me this: if you were to get it to a point where it is commercializable, you would need human test subjects, right?! Okay, well, *I* will be your first one, but off the books!"

"What are you playing at, Harvey?" Jeff's voice was wary, distrustful. "If this is a cheap ploy to get me to make some sort of admission, it won't work."

"Look, man, I had two clients today who told me they wanted me to completely redo their suits, for completely imbecilic reasons! One guy said the stripes didn't match up exactly perfectly. Like *ho-ly fuck!*" Harvey paced in circles in the small garage, his body language wild and agitated. "My boss is a prick, my coworkers are morons, and... and... and my wife is a goddamned dope fiend, and my kids are total brats... I just, I just..." he suddenly deflated with an immense sigh.

"I just don't have a lot going for me right now, so if I can help our great nation through the furthering of the scientific endeavour, it will have been pretty much the only useful contribution I will have ever made to society. I... I want to have that feeling... The feeling of finally being *useful.*" Harvey hung his head. Significantly uncomfortable with this emotional display, Jeff gave him a manly clap on the back and squeezed his shoulder ruggedly.

"Uh, it's okay, buddy! Things will get better with, uh... with everything! But, uh, look... if it will make you feel better, I promise you'll be first on the list when we get this thing up and running."

"So you *do* have something??"

"Well, I... yeah... yeah. We have figured out how to essentially combine cryogenics with minification – the extreme cold of the cryogenics offsets the problem of thermodynamic energy we were facing before. But it's not 100% A lot of the test animals have frozen to death. The cryogenics works initially, but when the minification starts, their vitals raise just enough so that they succumb to the extreme cold before anyone has an opportunity to realize what is happening. Some are cooked internally, but are still popsicles on the outside. With others, it's the opposite. But we're working on it. I'll let you know when we're ready for human testing."

"Thanks, Jeff. You're a good friend."

– 128 Days Later –

click – whirrrr – click

[Hey, you've reached Harvey Wienberg and family – please leave a message... *BEEP*]

"Uh, hey Harv, it's Jeff... Uh... I just wanted to let you know that we're ready for you... here... so, uh, just – "

click "H-Hello? Hello?? *Jeff?!*"

"Uh, Harv, hi –"

"Okay, great! When; what time; where?!"

"Uh, well, we've gotta do this at night, obviously, so just come to the back gate tomorrow, I guess – how about 1 am? ... Come on foot so that – "

"I need my car."

"Oh – uh, no, that's not ideal – why?"

"I have sprained my ankle and cannot walk long distances."

"Well, are you sure you want to go through with this, then? We can wait until you feel –"

"**NO!!** I'll be fine. I'll keep the lights of my car off so I won't attract attention."

"Well... okay, Harv... I'll see you tomorrow ni–"

SLAM

"...Harv?? Hello?? Jesus..."

click

...

The night was as black and cold as death unadulterated. Harvey Weinberg shivered in his midsized family sedan. He was hunched over the steering wheel, peering past the blue sun strip at the top of the windshield, up at the tall gate in front of him, topped with both razor and barbed wire. Inside the complex, he could see large dogs roaming around hungrily, just waiting for him to fuck up and give them their first meal in days.

The blinking red light at the top of the gate abruptly turned a solid green. The gate slid open with the grinding noise of metal rolling on metal. With a lurch, Harvey accelerated through the gate and down the long descending platform which spiralled down multiple rotations to a level which must have been several stories subground.

There he parked close to the door to the stairs. Through the little window he could see Jeff waiting for him; he opened the door as Harvey approached.

"Okay, follow me – " Jeff said, and began to ascend the stairwell.

"No!" Harvey stood completely still, an anxious look on his face. Jeff sighed wearily and turned back, his posture heavy. "*What??* What now, Harv?"

Harvey's face was white, and glistened with cold sweat.

"Jesus, are you okay, Harv? Do you have a flu or – "

"I – I need you to help me." Harvey stated, then abruptly turned and walked, rapidly and stiffly, back to his car. There he stood by the trunk, waiting impatiently, his fingers neurotically fiddling with his keys. Jeff slowly approached him, the hair on the back of his neck raising eerily. *Something is wrong... He's... he's walking just fine!*

Shrink Your Dead!

He stood there, as Harvey fumbled with the keys, dropping them twice, before opening the trunk. As the lid ascended slowly, Jeff yelled in terror, and stumbled backwards, tripping over his own feet. He lay there on the concrete, under the green flickering glow of the fluorescent lighting in the empty underground carpark, staring up at the lip of the trunk, at Harvey, hunched there, over the boot, looking sick and ghoulish. From the underside of the rear bumper, Jeff watched a single drop of blood gradually gather into a bead and fall in slow motion onto his sock, a striking crimson against the blinding white cotton. It rested there for a moment before soaking in, the perfect circle expanding outwards hungrily.

He unsteadily climbed to his feet. What he saw in the trunk made him gag, and heave onto the concrete. Harvey stared down into the black opening with wide, serious eyes, his hands trembling.

The inside of the trunk was completely saturated with blood. The carpeted floor was glistening and squishy with moisture. The roof and sides were streaked, splattered, and smeared. Inside the deep, yawning space, curled up seemingly in each other's arms, lay the bodies of two little children, a boy and a girl. Their eyes stared wildly up at Jeff, their faces frozen in their last horrible moments of agony and terror. Their throats had been cut almost to their spinal cords. Jeff could see the hard white rings of their severed tracheas.

He looked up at Harvey with wide, white eyes, then, overcome by a wave of vertigo, he fell onto the ground again, where he felt the strong need to curl up in a ball. He vomited again, hacking violently, his eyes crushed shut. Spitting, he sat up again, and a wave of cold washed over him. His eyes were watering; all he could see were blurry streaks of light and muddy colours. Yet, he could hear Harvey's voice coming from somewhere far away.

"...e need to get them inside, and Shannon, too."

"*Shannon?!*" Jeff cried. He crawled to his hands and knees, and by sheer willpower, clambered to the passenger side door of the car, and opened it. The body of a woman fell out, onto him, then over him, to land heavily upon its face on the concrete.

Gingerly, Jeff rolled Shannon over. Her face was a swollen purple and red mess; blood oozed from multiple blunt-trauma impact points. Her skull had several bizarre-looking indentations. He wouldn't have even recognized her, if he hadn't known.

Oh, Jesus...!!!

"Just, uh... you – you just wait here, Harv!" Jeff stammered, stumbling to the door of the stairwell. *I have to call the police! He's gone completely mad!!*

"**JEFF. STOP.**" The ice in Harvey Wienberg's voice halted Jeff cold in his tracks. He could hear the low, rhythmic percussion of his blood pounding in his ears. He wanted to run, but found, in his panic, he was glued to the spot. So, he stayed absolutely still, and listened to the sound of footsteps approaching from behind him. Then, he heard, in his right ear, his own voice.

"... *figured out how to essentially combine cryogenics with minification – the extreme cold of the cryogenics offsets the problem of thermodynamic energy we were facing before. But it's not...*"

The tape stopped with a click, like the sound of a pistol hammer being thumbed back.

"I... I'm sorry, but I *need* your help with this. **Right now.** I'm really sorry, Jeff. I'll explain everything when we get somewhere we can talk – but first, we *need* to take care of this!"

Slowly, Jeff turned around, his vision a long, hazy tunnel, and walked dizzily back to the car.

...

"I'm not crazy, Jeff. Really. Not anymore. I *was.* You would have been, too, if you had to endure what I did, every day. Bratty little assholes for kids. A drug-addicted zombie of a wife who couldn't even wipe her own drool. A job beneath a megalomaniac boss who loathes me, alongside coworkers I despise. Every day, the same thing. For *years.* It was enough to crack even the toughest man, which I'm not, obviously."

The two men stood in the middle of Jeff's lab, leaning on shimmering stainless steel counters. Harvey was quarter way though a bottle of scotch Jeff had been saving for a special occasion. This was as good as any – maybe he would drink himself into a state where he could easily be subdued, or, even better, pass out on his own. But he seemed extraordinarily lucid.

"You *need* me, Jeff. We can work together. You need a competent tailor. I need a docile, obedient, loving family, the sort my grandfather valued! I need to be the *man* of my own house! You CAN do this. You said so yourself. You can install the moving parts, and the software, and the hardware, and certain... anatomical modifications, and shrink us all – my children, my wife, and I. We can live in the full-featured dollhouse created for extended human miniaturization trials. Tell them it fell from the table and was smashed, and you'll just build a new one. You can bring this one home; set it up with all the amenities, and my family and I will live in it. In return, I will make custom outfits for you, to such a level of detail your coworkers will be in awe. 'What tailor do you use??' they will ask you with wide eyes, and you will just smile and remain silent as the grave."

Jeff shuddered at the turn of phrase. He was not feeling much better than he had in the car park. They had stuffed Harvey's family into body bags and dragged them up six flights of stairs. He could still hear the hollow

Shrink Your Dead!

thunk, thonk* of the children's skulls as they bounced off the concrete stairs, one after the other... off all 72 steps.

"We can work together!" grinned Harvey, exuberantly. "Otherwise I'll be *forced* to confess that you revealed classified information, and ruin your career. I'd rather not. It was just a bargaining chip. I didn't ever want to have to use it. You're still my friend, Jeff." Harvey suddenly drew very close to the taxidermist. His breath was hot and damp and reeked with alcohol, mere millimeters from Jeff's face. His eyes were wide and wild. He hissed excitedly:

"**BE** my friend, Jeff! Bring my dream to life! Give me my perfect family! ... I've been waiting for so long..."

Jeff swallowed hard, and looked over at the operating tables, where the three lumpy black sacks lay. His spine was buckled, his breathing shallow. When he spoke, his voice was barely a whisper:

"Okay, Harv... I'll do it..."

...

Harvey Wienberg softly kisses the top of Sally's head, and runs his fingers through her silky, blonde hair. *Finally, she's fallen asleep.*

He pads back to his bedroom. Shannon lies, unmoving, exactly as he had left her. He climbs into bed and runs his fingertips hungrily over her cold breasts, those perpetually hard nipples.

"Honey, I'm ready again if you are..." he croons to her, running his tongue over his teeth lustily. He taps a unique combination of buttons into the control unit on his wrist. From deep within the inky blackness of Shannon's motionless lips, drifts an adoring, obsequious female voice.

"Oh, you can have me *any* old time... I *live* for you, darling... You were amazing, dear!"

[2016-01-24 /03:58:00]

One Thread Short

Bentley McKinnon is my brother, and he's a retard.

It's because of the water tower. I seen it with my own two eyes, cuz I was there. He even got a big ol' dent in his head. It's in the left side above his ear and it looks like someone took a big scoop out of his head with a big ol' spoon.

When he was little, Bentley was pretty normal like me or any other boy. But when he was eleven (I was seven) we was all playing Cowboys n' Injuns out in the back corn field by the big red cow barn with the creaky rooster weather vane up on the top of it.

I remember it was just after Halloween, and the corn harvest was about halfway done; and the northeast field was just all fulla tall corn stalks, taller'n your head, but no corn (if we got caught playing in the fields that ain't been harvested yet, we'd shurly get a whuppin'), and me'n the other boys would play there. The injuns would hide and the cowboys would come after 'em, and if they found one, the injun would run n' a cowboy would chase 'im, looking to get a bead on him with his six-shooter, but if an injun managed to surprise a cowboy, the cowboy'd have to run, cuz the injun would scalp'im with his tomahawk.

It was just before dinner, and the sun was just going down behind the Guadalupe Peak mountains, making long golden beams of light shafting through the corn stalks – the air was so dusty you could actually see the light rays, it was swell to look at, but not when you're running like a fresh-branded filly away from an injun, which is what Bentley was doing. Now, at the southeast corner of the southeast corn field is a big ol' water tower, and the bottom of it is all four legs encased in concrete with sharp square edges. Bentley was running like to save his life from a cowboy, and he was looking back over his right shoulder when he burst outa the corn and charged right into one of those concrete legs, like a blinded bull. He was going so fast he was windmilling and when he hit that concrete, the side of his head hit the sharp edge, and it seemed to keep going a little, before it bounced back with a sound like when you chuck a rotten egg at the ground to watch it explode.

Bentley just sorta pitched right back like a wobbly domino and hit the ground and lay there. It was a real shock cuz he had been hollering something fierce, and the moment he hit the leg of that water tower he stopped hollering like someone had cut off his head, and instead started twitching and flailing on the ground, making noises like he was choking and gagging. Pretty quick after that, though, he just stopped moving and making noise altogether. I was standing over him, looking down on him with my hands on my knees, breathing hard, cuz it was me was the cowboy chasin'im, and the side of his head was all pushed in, and was bleeding so much it was like when you turn a garden hose on real gentle-like, then hold it straight up so it makes a soft little fountain of water all down over itself – that's what

One Thread Short

Bentley's head was doing. It made me feel queer to watch it, but a'course I didn't watch it for long, cuz I was hollering my own head off, calling for somebody to come quick, cuz my big brother Bentley McKinnon had just killed his fool self.

Course, he hadn't killed hisself. But he came real close. I had to help the doc fix him up in the kitchen of our house, and there was an actual crack in his head which fit just right to the sharp corner of the water tower leg, and the doc kinda reached in with the flat handle of a spoon, and pulled the skull out again so that it wasn't so much poking into Bentley's brain, which I could see with my own two eyes, but even after he did it, there was still a big dent. Doc Martin (like the shoes) said he wanted to "leave wellenuff alone and only do what was absolutely nesissary to releeve the presher on the brain." (sorry if that ain't right, but I can't spell to good.) So he bandaged up Bentley's head real tight, and actually stayed right there in our house, 'cept for when he had to take the old Ford to somebody else's house cuz they were sick or whatever, but he always come back.

After a week, he said he was pretty sure Bentley would live, said he was real scared he wouldn't, but he also said he didn't think it would be much of a life, if'n he ever did wake up from the coma he was in. Our Ma was crying, and Pa was standing there with his arms crossed, and his lips were a real straight line across, and white around the edges, and he was nodding his head and saying "Mmmhmm, Mmmhmm." over and over, like he was fillosofizing real hard about it.

...

Well, Bentley eventually did wake up, cuz if he didn't, I wouldn't be telling this story, a'course. (Well, maybe I woulda been, but it woulda stopped right there, and it's not.) So, he woke up right around Christmas, and Mrs. Jensen the pastor's wife swore it was a present from the baby Jesus. But it was real odd, cuz the Bentley that woke up weren't the same Bentley we'd all known before. For starters, he couldn't say nothing. He just made stupid noises like a sick cow, and he drooled all the time, and his eyes never opened more'n half way, and, well, he had turned into a retard real good. You could say he's one thread short of a spool.

So, before the accident, he was always working on the farm with Pa, and I was just learning, but then after the accident, he couldn't do nothing, and it was me had always to be shovelling pig manure and chicken shit, which, teknikaly, are the same sort of thing, but if you ever been ankle-deep in both of 'em, you can see right away they ain't the same thing no how.

So I liked him a lot less after the accident just cuzza that, and it seemed like Pa was the same way, cuz he had been looking forward to both Bentley and me helping on the farm, and now he just had another mouth to feed that didn't do nothing. For a while Ma cried about him and tried to help him get normal again, but then she got sick and didn't spend any more time on him until she died.

So nobody all that much liked new Bentley, except my little brother, Mickey, who was only two when it happened, so he never knew the old Bentley, but he knows this one better'n anyone. I'm sixteen now, and he's eleven, and he spends all his time with that mute. He reads to'im and feeds'im and stuff, but the thing is, though, I'm real sore about Mickey, to, cuz he never has to do any farm work, neither. He got a bum leg from being born, and he can't walk to good. He can't even do easy stuff like picking eggs cuz he stomps all round with his bad leg and scares all the chickens. Our Pa calls'im Gimpy. Even says it to his face, and Mickey, he might just stare down at his plate if it's dinner time, and stir his peas around with his spoon and not say anything, and I don't really know what he's thinking, but he gets pretty quiet after that for a while. I think he likes Bentley cuz they're both retards.

Today I see him what looks like tryna teach Bentley how to write, as I walk by the door to his room in the upstairs hallway. Mickey sees me and calls me in.

"Hey, Fletcher, check this out!" he says. "Bentley can use me to speak!"

"What? Are you dumb, Mick?? Bentley can't talk, not since the accident."

"Well, not speak, actually, but write. He uses my hand."

"What the hell d'you mean?"

"See, his primary and secondary motor cortices got all messed up on the left side, so he can't write properly with his right hand, which was his dominant hand to begin with. I think it also has to do with his Broca's aphasia, which is why he can't speak."

Now, this pisses me off. I ain't never gone to school or nothing, cuz Pa always kept me back to work on the farm, so I don't know what the hell he's talking about. None of the other kids can follow him neither, even the ones who *do* go to school. I heard Billy Marten's mother talking with Rodd Silverstein's mother. She works in the library, and she brings Mickey books every week, cuz he can't get down there on account of not being able to walk or ride a bike. She said he asks for university textbooks, and that he's "prekoshus", whatever that means. I guess it must mean that he's really smart, and I'm pretty sure he says all that smart crap to me to rub it in that I'm real dumb, so it pisses me off!

"Oh, shut the hell up, Gimpy!" I holler at him. "Who cares about that stuff?" Mickey scowls a moment, but then he bites his lip and looks patiently up at me, like I'm a goddamn moron.

"Sorry, I get carried away. All I mean is that he can't speak or write because of the accident, so he has to borrow my hand to write."

"Whattaya mean "borrow"?" (I gotta admit, I wanna know what he means, cuz then I can feel less dumb.)

"Well, I go like this... I sit here at the desk, and Bentley sits next to me, and I put his hand over top of mine, with the pencil in my hand, like I'm gonna write something, see?"

Bentley makes a retarded noise and drools on the paper. "Uhhh, yeah, I see somethin'." I say.

"Then I close my eyes," Mickey goes on, "and I clear my mind, so I can hopefully sync my neural waves to his, since we're so close, and I let him use my hand to write something. He can only ever write one word, though."

I still feel stupid, and I'm getting' hot under my collar, cuz I think Mickey is playin' me for a fool.

"What? Show me!" I demand. So he does just what he said: he closes his eyes, and a moment later, he writes something on the paper. Then he opens his eyes and looks up at me.

"See, I don't even know what he wrote. I can tell my hand is moving, but I'm not controlling it."

We both peer at the paper. On it I see written:

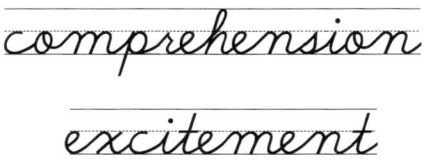

I can't figure out what that says; I never learned to read squiggly writing! I'm about to deck Mickey for making an ass of me, but then he tells me what the words are, and that the first one was from before I came in the room. Then I really do deck him; I give him a Charley Horse in the shoulder, and Bentley starts howling like a retarded caveman and waving his arms about. I ignore him.

"You stinkin' jerk!" I yell at Mickey, "You're makin' all that stuff up! You're just writin' whatever you feel like and makin' up a story to make me look stupid!"

"No... I'm serious..." says Mickey, wincing in pain and rubbing his shoulder. "I'll prove it. I'll go out of the room – I'll even go outside so you can see me out the window and that I'm not listening in outside the door, and you tell Bentley some random word, and I'll come in and let him use my hand to write it. I guarantee you it will be the right word."

I don't know why I go along with it, but I do. Mickey goes outside and waves at me from the mud patch that is our backyard, and I look over at Bentley McKinnon, who's staring at me with his half-closed idiot's eyes, and dripping drool down off his chin onto the carpet. "Okay, retard, listen up." I tell him, and whisper a word to him. Then I holler out the window at Mickey, and he comes up and does the thing again. When he's done, written in the notebook is:

"Bullshit." says Mickey.

"*WHAT!?*" I yell. "AIN'T NO WAY! YOU MUSTA **GUESSED!!**" Mickey looks irritated.

"Hey, if you don't believe me, why don't you try it yourself?" He gets up out of the wooden chair, and offers it to me, but I've had enough of this crap. I'm steamin' mad and my cheeks are burning, and my fingernails are hurting my palms cuz I'm clenching my fists so bad, and I figger I better leave before I sock Mickey in the head and maybe turn him out like Bentley, so I storm outta the room and slam the door.

Later, we're eating dinner (Mickey, Pa, Bentley and me) and Pa is in a mood. He's kinda always been in a mood, since Ma died, back when I was eleven. Doc Martin says she had cancer – a brain tumour – he done some X-rays 'fore she died, cuz she was getting migraine headaches all the time, and then one day she went totally blind. Doc Martin said she had a tumour the size of a golf ball beneath the part of the brain that she uses to see, in back of her head, and it was pressing on that part and broke it. We couldn't afford surgery, though, so she just kept getting worse, and then one day she just didn't wake up. Doc Martin said that the part of the brain beneath the tumour controlled her breathing and heartbeat, and the tumour broke that part too, so she stopped breathing and heartbeating.

Pa got real broke up about it, and he started spending all his extra money on whiskey n' scotch' n' rum. He kind of was spending the *not*-extra money, too, since we got our telephone and our electricity and our television cut off, since he didn't never pay'em. He would just drink and yell and throw stuff, and he lots of times thumped me around somethin' good. Still does, even...

Anyway, we're at the table eating dinner, which is potatoes, which is all we've had for dinner for about three weeks, cuz the crops are failing on account'a a real long drought, and I'm trying not to gag as it sticks in my throat. Pa is telling Mickey he's not going back to school next month, in September, cuz he's got to help out with the farm or we'll all starve. As it is we lost all the crops 'cept for a couple acres of wheat and corn, and we gotta save that to sell. Mickey says that he can't help cuz of his leg, and Pa said that things are harder now and everybody got to pull their weight. Then Mickey says a real stupid thing: he says that there ain't nothin' he can do to make it rain, and did Pa expect him to dance?

Pa says that he'll dance, alright, and he jumps up, and his chair flies over backwards, and he grabs Mickey by the back of the collar, and pulls *his* chair over backwards, and Mick's feet kick the bottom of the table on his way down and spills the water glasses. Pa's got Mickey by the front of the shirt with both his fists, and he's calling him a cocky, spoiled little shit, and pumping him up and down, slamming his shoulders back against the dusty hardwood floor, and lifting him up, and slamming him back down again, and Mickey's got his eyes real wide, staring at Pa, and his teeth are clenched and he looks like he's shitting bricks. His legs are kicking in the air, and I feel bad for him, cuz I know what it's like, and I can't decide if I should try to pull Pa off him or not, cuz my nose has just set from a couple weeks ago when he socked it, and I don't really want him to hit it again and break it again.

Just then Bentley starts screaming, and he makes a big movement with his arms across the table, sweeping most of the dishes onto the floor with a terrible smash. Pa gets off Mickey right quick and goes to whelp Bentley, but he stops short, prolly on account of him seeing the dent in Bentley's head, and remembering that if he socked him, he'd prolly die. So he just yells and hollers and waves his arms in the air and throws a plate at the wall, saying "Let's just fuckin' break all the fuckin' dishes!" but he doesn't throw any more after that. Instead, he storms off muttering to himself, and I know he's off to his liquor cabinet, to get a bottle and his cigarettes, and go out onto the back porch to drink and smoke, which means we'll be okay in here for about an hour, until he gets real hammered and comes back in to rampage.

I help Mickey up, and without a word, we clean up the mess. Bentley has gone up to his room, and halfway through cleaning up, Mickey just turns and hobbles upstairs. I figure maybe he wants to go into his room and cry a bit (which I get, cuz I usually have to do that after a lickin' from Pa) so I let him alone and keep washing the dishes. After a few minutes, though, I hear a ruckus coming from upstairs, so I wander over to listen up.

I hear Mickey yelling:

"NO! I **WON'T!!** I'M NOT GOING TO!!"

Then he comes storming down the stairs as fast as he can, and hobbles out of the front door into the dark. I call after him, but he don't listen, and I'm about to go after him, when I hear Bentley upstairs, screaming like a lunatic and trashing his room – I can hear the shelf knocked over, and other stuff being thrown around. I run upstairs to try to get him to stop before Pa hears, but I don't know what to do to stop him, he's just so retarded and I can't get through to him. So then I run back downstairs and out the door, and I'm yelling Mickey's name, but he ain't answering. I run to the barn, but he's not there, and I check the henhouse and everywhere else I can think of, but he ain't anyplace. I start getting real worried, cuz Mickey's a little too soft and gimpy to be running around outside at night, and the air smells angry, like a storm's brewin'.

Well, I'm getting' real steamed, cuz I figger this is all Bentley's fault, cuz he must have tried to get Mickey to do something he didn't wanna do, which got him upset and then he ran away. So I charge back inside just as fast as I can, and up the stairs, and I see Bentley sitting in his room at his desk, totally silent and still, like he's not even home. I come in and shove him, and he almost falls off the chair, and it startles the sense back in him, and he looks at me with wider eyes n'usual, and starts hooting and squealing like he's tryna say something. He grabs the notebook off the desk and throws it at me. I dodge it and pick it up off the floor and have a look at the last thing written in it:

don't

stop!

It takes me a real long time, but I finally figure out what it says, by using the set of flash cards Mickey made when he was trying to teach me how to write squiggly letters, so I kinda decoded the words with'em.

Don't stop!

What the hell is that supposed to mean?! I get real pissed off on account of thinkin' so hard, and I grab Bentley by the shirt and start shaking him and yelling at him.

"What did you do to him?! *Where is he?!*" I scream, but Bentley just looks at me real serious-like, in a way he's never looked at me before, and it kinda creeps me out, cuz for the first time since the accident, he doesn't have on his retard-eyes. It's like he's wearing someone else's eyes, and they're looking right through me.

He quite suddenly grabs the pencil off the desk and actually gives it to me, which is the most coordinated and purposeful thing I've ever seen him do. His teeth are clenched and it looks like he's concentrating real hard.

So I take the pencil from him and stare at it in my hand, then I stare at him, staring at me. I get to thinking that I'm worried enough about Mickey that I'll try anything if it means I'll find him.

"Okay then, tell me where he is." I whisper, and I sit down at the desk. I put Bentley's hand over mine and put the tip of the pencil on the page. I close my eyes and try to think of nothing and do whatever Mickey said he did with his brain, but instead, I just think,

I can't believe I'm doing this crap.

Well, just start scribbling something, and see what happens, I tell myself. So I do. I just move my hand in random, meaningless directions, and I'm totally convinced I'm gonna see just a mess like this:

But instead what I see is this:

Lightning

I can't even believe it, but as I'm staring at it with my mouth open, tryna make sense of it, a peal of thunder booms and rolls across the sky like a giant rolling over in bed, echoing off the edges of the sky in every direction. It is so gigantic it freezes me in my step, and then, all at once, a torrent of rain pours out of the sky, and I'm blinded by a brilliant flash of light outside. For that brief moment, I see something strange, and I peer into the darkness. I hear Pa down on the balcony outside, yelling with joy about the rain, but I'm too upset to care.

The field directly out back of the house is fallow – on account of the drought, nothin'll grow in it, so it's just ploughed dirt hoping to gain enough nutrients to grow something once the drought ends for good. I see a little figure far in the distance, hobbling through the field, and I know right away that it's Mickey, running who knows where, but now he's in a real dangerous situation. It's no use yelling out the window at him, the rain and wind is too loud, and he's too far away.

I'm just about to run out after him, when another bolt of lightning comes shooting down out of the sky, all crackly and crinkly, like a straight line that's been crumpled up like paper, then uncrumpled, and now it looks all bent and ragged. It reaches down out of the clouds and stabs the tiny figure in the middle of the field like a spear. There is a flash of static, and sparks, and then the ground is on fire, cuz there's old dead grass all over the field, and something else is on fire, and I know it is Mickey, lying there in the dirt.

One Thread Short

I don't care about the lightning, I just run outside and through the field, and I slip and fall in the mud a few times, but I finally get to the burning lump in the middle of it, and it is Mickey, and his shirt and pants are on fire, but the rain has drowned it, and now it's just smoking. I see in the flash of another lightning burst that his hair is smoking, and I don't know if he's alive, but I scoop him up over my shoulder and hightail it outta there. On the way back, I slip and fall again, and I accidentally dump Mickey in the mud, face down. As I scramble to my feet, I look up to find Pa beside me, picking him up. We run into the house, and even though I know Pa is hammered, he runs straight, and drops Mickey on the couch. He puts his ear to Mickey's chest, and then makes a horrible anguished noise, before climbing on top of him and clasping both his fists together and raising them up and smashing them down on Mickey's chest so hard I'm certain he's gonna break his ribs, but then the thought occurs to me that if this means what I think it means, a broken rib ain't gonna do no pain to my little brother Mickey McKinnon. I hold my breath.

In between, Pa keeps pushing on Mick's chest in short rhythmic bursts, but after a few minutes, he collapses on top of Mickey and starts sobbing and wailing like I ain't never seen him do, since Ma died. I glance over at the old rotary telephone, thick with dust. We ain't got no telephone service, so I can't call Doc Martin. I tell Pa I'll go ride to the neighbour's and use their phone, but he looks up at me from the chair he's just sat in, and he's sagging, like a wet scarecrow, and he makes a limp, lifeless gesture, like a scarecrow in the wind, and he says, "Don't bother... don't bother..." just like that, and he puts his head in his hands. Then he abruptly stands up and goes back outside to where I know his bottle of whiskey is waiting for him. The rain keeps on pouring, but he ain't happy about it no more. Instead, it just brought sadness.

...

A few days later, Pa and Bentley and I are gathered in the cemetery in behind the little church in town, and so are a couple dozen other families, come to pay their respects to Mickey. He looks all nice in his coffin, all dressed up in the suit he used to have to wear on Sundays, back when Pa believed in going to church. This is kinda funny, cuz Mickey just hated wearing that suit, and he was so glad when we stopped going. It makes me think it's kinda stupid and unfair to Mick, and that he ought to have been buried in his ripped jeans and his favourite Flash Gordon t-shirt and his torn sneakers, cuz then he'd'a been more comfortable.

I brung his knobby wooden cane from home, and I put it in the coffin beside him. I stare down at the kid, and I don't know what to say to him, so I just slug him in the shoulder like I used to do when I was playing with him, or when I was mad at him, but I'm not mad at him right now; I just don't know what else to do, so now I walk away and go sit on a tombstone across the cemetery, and pull some small stones outta my jacket pockets and start chuckin'em at a cross with a circle around the middle, but I keep missing.

"I'm real sorry 'bout your brother, Fletch," says a voice. I look up. It's Nina Winterfield, who is Zack Winterfield's kid sister, and they live a couple farms down. She is fourteen and a half, which is two years younger'n me, and she looks real pretty in her white dress with little purple flowers all over it, and her shiny Mary Jane shoes with the silver buckle. She has blonde hair that is so light it's almost white, and it's bunched up on her head all nice in a way I can't describe, but it's nice. I'm surprised to see her like that, cuz usually her long hair is all messy and down over her shoulders. I ain't never seen her neck before. Her throat is very smooth and long and curvy, like the way water looks when it goes down a softly flowing creek. Her jaw is a real sharp angled line, and her ears are super tiny. I ain't never seen'em before, not like this. Usually, her hair is all tangled up and she's all dirty and wearing scrubs like I am, cuz she's a farm girl like I am – I mean, uh... Anyway, she looks *beautiful*, and I start to get hot in my cheeks, and suddenly I'm thinking I want to steal Nina Winterfield away into the hayloft in my barn and take off all her clothes and look at her naked body and her soft cat fur, and breathe the sweet rich scent of her poozle, and then I'd...

"Why you lookin' at me that way, Fletch?" She asks, and her voice is softer, curiouser'n usual.

"Oh, sorry, just thinking." I say, embarrassed. I stand up and turn away, afraid she'll see that I suddenly got a rocket. She doesn't say nothing, and I don't say nothing, and only the wind says something, and it all of a sudden sounds real loud, so I turn around cuz I managed to sneakily shift my knob so it's tucked up under my belt buckle, and I say:

"So, uh, how's your Girl Scouts goin'?" and I know I sound as dumb as I really am, but I can't thinka nothin' else to say, and it's better than sayin' nothin' at all.

"Oh... y'know, I ain't really like them other girls, all talkin' about makeup and when the next Beatles album's gonna come out, and which one is the cutest, and how many acres does Ringo's nose cover, and nonsense like that, y'know?" She picks up a stone and, with a casual flick, chucks it right through the hole in the cross I've been tryna score in this whole time. "I don't wanna sell cookies, I wanna catch toads n' squirrels..." she says, sounding real sad and real frustrated at the same time.

I nod, silently. I get it.

"You look real nice," I say, kinda embarrassed. "Real pretty. I ain't never seen you with your hair up. Looks nice."

Nina Winterfield blushes and looks down at her hands. "I think it looks stupid. Ain't nobody'd ever kiss a plain, ugly girl like me, not even when I get all dolled up like a trollop."

One Thread Short

I don't know what that is, but I ain't gonna admit that to Nina. "Aww, naww, you know... I bet lotsa boys'd like ta kiss ya." I say, feeling like my ears are too big.

She shrugs and looks away, making me feel pretty stupid for saying something like that. Then, she makes it even worse by saying:

"Well, I'm gonna go... I'll see ya 'round, Fletch..." and she says it without even looking up at me, then turns and walks back to the group of people around the grave. I watch her go. I watch her dress as it gathers round her legs with every step, wrapping itself around them and touching her, all the way up those long legs, like I wanna do, all the way up to...

I shiver and shake the image out of my head, and go back to chucking pebbles at the cross. I shouldn't think of Nina like that. It just makes me feel even dumber n' uglier than I already do.

...

I'm surprised to see her again a couple days later. It's late in the afternoon, getting round dinner time, and I'm just finishing binding and stooking three acres of grain. I gotta first use the tractor rigged with the harvester to cut the sheaves of wheat, and it gathers and spits out little piles of raw wheat every few feet. Then I gotta gather all those piles and stand 'em up on end and bind 'em together into stooks, so they can easily be collected for threshing. It was scorching hot today, and I got my shirt off and I'm dripping with sweat, and covered in wheat dust that's flying all over the place.

I just finished binding a stook and I straighten up and wipe the sweat outta my eyes. I'm dead tired, and my feet hurt, and I'm looking forward to dinner. Suddenly, I'm surprised by a voice, just like at the funeral, coming outta nowhere and startling me.

"Hey, Fletch, how's the wheat comin' along?"

I spin around and see Nina there, looking more like I'm used'ta seeing her, in dirty, torn blue jean coveralls, a long-sleeved red checkered shirt, and her yellow-silver hair, all messy and tangled and fulla little bits of grass n' stuff, where it isn't covered by her cowboy hat. Her face has lotsa dirt all over it, and she's sitting on the wooden fence by the property line, chewing her nails. I don't feel nervous seeing her like this, cuz she just looks like one of the boys, like usual.

"Oh, 'bout done," I say, squinting into the evening sun. Then there's a moment of silence, cuz I can't think of anything else to say, just cuz there's nothing else to say. Nina smirks and hops off the fence and walks over to me.

"I just finished choppin', cleanin', and sortin' about half a thousand husks'a corn for market this week. Thought I'd come by here... want some help with them stooks?" she asks.

One Thread Short

"Well, shore," I say, and we spend the next half hour doing what it woulda taken me an hour to do by myself. The whole time, we're talking about nothing, but it feels like we're talking about *everything*, even though I can't explain what I mean by that. She says she's planning on catching some frogs so she can roast the legs over a fire, and I say I'm planning on picking the thimbleberries out back the henhouse, so Gramma Pratt down the way can make some fresh berry pie, and she'll gimme one for my trouble.

We talk about school, about how I don't go and she does; I say I'm real jealous of her, but she says I ought not to be, cuz her grades are awful, n' her Ma is the Primary teacher, so she tans her hide pretty regular when she comes home with bad marks. She says she shore ain't looking forward to school starting again in the fall. Thing is, she says, she's trying real hard, but she gots a problem with seeing numbers and letters, like they flip upside down and backwards sometimes for no reason, and it's real hard to make them sense like that, but she don't wanna tell nobody 'bout it, cuz she's afraid they'll say she's retarded and put her in the slow class. So instead, she just acts like she don't give a shit about it, like she failed the examinations on purpose, cuz she don't care, cuz it's better than being thought of as retarded. But she actually cares a whole lot.

Her voice is real strange as she's talking 'bout that, as we sit by the barn n' drink fresh clear water outta the well. She talks real quiet, and she's looking at the ground the whole time, and when she looks up, I'm startled to see she's crying a little. I don't know what to say, so I just pat her awkwardly on the shoulder, but she suddenly throws her arms round me and squeezes me real tight. This makes my heart beat real fast, and I find I can't breathe to good, so I'm kinda gulping as I try to tell her that I feel pretty retarded mosta the time, to. I tell her I feel pretty much jealous of Bentley, cuz at least he gots a excuse, where with me, I'm just a dumb farm boy who's gonna just only be a dumb farm man for all my life, and that's about it.

She smiles through her tears and tells me I ain't so dumb, at least I can read n' write, and I tell her just barely, and it's only on account'a Mickey teaching me, and as I say it, my voice suddenly cracks and my sight gets all smeary, cuz I'm thinking about Mickey, and how I ain't never gonna see him no more, and my eyes are devilish hot and I'm crying and feeling even stupider'n usual, but Nina just hugs me again for a real long time, before Pa yells out the window where the hell am I and dinner ain't gonna cook itself, goddamnit!

So I say goodbye to Nina and go inside, and I'm real quiet all evening, just thinking about it.

...

I end up spending the whole resta' the summer with Nina, and we go hunting for those frogs together, and pick those thimbleberries together, and eat that pie together, and we laugh real good at each other, cuz our faces are all purple with berry juice, cuz we're such messy eaters.

Then one evening, the sun is just hiding behind the spiky horizon of the forest behind the farm, and the mountains beyond that, and the sky is a real deep pink right by the bottom, then it blends into a deep purple, then dark blue farther up. It's real nice.

I'm just finishing picking eggs outta the henhouse, and I'm in the barn, rinsing them off in a bucket of water, when Nina appears behind me like she always does, and startles the bejeezus outta me. I think I must be the deafest person in the world that she can always sneak up on me like that.

"Oh, hey, Nina," I say, and I wipe my wet hands on the fronta my shirt.

"Fletcher…" she says real quiet-like, looking at the buttons of my shirt, and I realize just then how short she is, cuz she's looking at my third button from the top but she's looking straight ahead.

"Yeah?" I say.

"You said before how you think I'm real pretty and you bet a lotta guys wanna kiss me." She says, chewing on her bottom lip, then licking it, which makes it glisten and shine in the golden light of the lantern.

"Mmmhmm," I say, feeling weird.

She suddenly shuffles right up next to me, and I stiffen all up and get all tingly in my fingertips, cuz I'm not expecting it.

"You wanna kiss me, Fletch?" she whispers, her breath wet in my ear, and it makes me shiver, and the thought of kissing Nina Winterfield gives me a rocket straightaway.

"Uh, shore, yeah, I guess so," I stammer, and now she's leaning up on her toes and wrapping her arms round my neck, and before I know it, I can feel her hot, moist, shiny lips on mine, and I can't barely breathe. She kisses me like that for a really long time, and she even puts her tongue in my mouth and backs me up against a pillar and actually rubs her crotch on my leg, and my hands are finding the curve of her spine right above her waist, and I feel her hooters against my chest and I damn near forgot she was shaped so much like a girl, since that time I seen her in that dress.

Then, just as quick as anything, she peels herself off me and, with a little blushing smile, runs off outta the barn, and I'm so focused on the sight of her leaving that I nearly have a heart attack when Blondie, our horse, neighs right in my ear and gums my cheek with her slobbery lips.

Seems like I'm pretty popular with the ladies tonight…

…

One Thread Short

So, the next day, I'm sitting at the desk in Bentley's room, and he's sitting next to me, drooling and looking as retarded as ever, but I'm staring at the notebook in fronta me, cuz I just done the thing with him borrowing my hand, like Mickey'd do, and I don't know what to think about what I'm seeing, which is this:

alive

"Who's alive?" I whisper.

mickey

"Bullshit," I hiss, afraid Pa'll hear me being a lunatic up here – I know I sure can't explain what I'm doing. I don't even know myself. So I close my eyes and think real hard and do the thing a buncha times without even looking, and when I do, I see:

water

sharp

hurt

red

black

white

death

life

"What the hell is that!" I seethe through my teeth, "Can't you talk normal and give me a goddamn sentence?" and Bentley clenches his jaw again and puts his hand back over mine. I close my eyes again, and this time I feel a weird feeling in my head, and behind my closed eyelids the blackness suddenly explodes into flashes of blues and reds, swirling like oil in a puddle, and then I'm scribbling again, fast, and when I look I see:

Take me to Bryce's Canyon.

...

At the canyon, the wind is hot, and it's tearing at my clothes. I squint against the summer sun, and look out over the cliff. It drops down a good hundred feet, but it's not a sheer drop, more like a V-shape, with bumps and outcroppings on the way down, and in the winter, there's a creek at the bottom, but it's dry now.

"Well, what now?" I ask Bentley. I'm tired, cuz I just put him in the old Radio Flyer wagon, and tied that to my bicycle, and then towed him all the way up here.

Bentley looks out into the canyon, and down the side, and he all of a sudden makes a big retarded noise like a chimpanzee, hooting for joy like it's his birthday or something, and he flails his arms all around just like a monkey.

Then he shoves me off the cliff.

The first thing I think is that I'm surprised he's so strong, then I hit the first outcropping with my shoulder, then the second with my cheekbone, and it rings my bell so hard I don't think anything after that – the world is just flashing yellow and red and spinning round and round. I hit my head again and everything goes black, and when I can see again, I'm still tumbling, faster 'n ever it seems, and the sky is spinning so quick I feel like hurling. Then I hit the bottom, and my head bounces off a rock, and I hear and feel a crunchy sound, which I'm pretty sure is my skull, and everything goes black again. A moment later I can see again, but it's all blurry and shaky, and I can't move my arms or my legs, and I see Bentley's body come crashing down beside me. The dent in his head has opened up again and I can see his brain pushing out through the hole. He doesn't look alive. I watch as my own blood pools out from I think my ear and is very shiny and red, then everything fades into black and I think, *that's it, I'm dead.*

...

But then the tiniest white dot appears in the middle of the darkness, and it gets bigger and bigger, until it is all I can see and I'm blinded by it. I crush my eyes shut; it's too bright, but then I hear a voice which I can't recognize.

"Brother, it's good to see you." I feel a hand on my shoulder. I open my eyes, expecting a sea of blood and Bentley's brain hole, but instead, I see a blue sky, and green trees and grass, and wild birds of variegated hues of scarlet, gold, jade, indigo, cerulean; they're flitting and fluttering about, singing in beautiful, superlative melodies. I sit up, shakily, and look around. I'm not in Bryce's Canyon, I'm in some sort of garden, like a jungle, almost, and all around are animals just resting – I see gazelle and jackals drinking together at a sparkling spring, I see a lion curled up, sleeping, with a fluffy white lamb. It's unreal. Then I look up.

Standing above me, offering me his hand, is... is Bentley McKinnon, my brother, but he is not a retard. He's strong and healthy and tall, and his eyes are clear and purposeful – the same other-person eyes I saw in the other Bentley. I take his hand and he easily pulls me up. He's not wearing a shirt, and his muscles are bulging. He has long sideburns and shaggy hair. His skull is the right shape. I'm surprised at how old he looks, and I remember that he *is* my big brother, but the accident produced the resultant appearance of vast immaturity, and I lost track of the fact that he's twenty years old now.

"It's been too long, Fletch, since I could talk to you properly," he says warmly. "And damn, it's good to be back!" He smiles and embraces me. I pat him on the back gingerly, awed and stupefied, and then I see other people surrounding us. I'm even more surprised to see Mickey, alive and well, looking better than ever, actually. He walks over to me – not hobbles, not limps, but walks – and also embraces me. After that, I see *my mother!* She looks gorgeous! Not pale and sickly and skinny and wrinkled like I remember her. She looks like an angel and smiles like one too, as she, too, hugs me. There are many other people, also, most of whom I don't recognize.

I'm overwhelmed.

"Is... is this heaven?" I stammer. Despite a desperate scouring of my faculties of logic, it's the only explanation that makes sense.

"Yes and no," says Mickey, eating fat blue-black grapes from a vine. "Ever heard of string theory?"

I'd usually think he's trying to boast his intellect and make me look contrastingly obtuse, but I don't feel that way, this time. He smiles a little at me.

"No, I haven't," I say, returning his calm smile.

"The multiverse theory states that there is not one universe, but multiple universes, connected through time and space by wormholes," he says. "Alternate realities, if you will. What we consider death is actually a wormhole to one of the dimensions directly... adjacent... to our own, if you will, although the dimensions aren't so simple. It's kind of like a tesseract. So, the "white light at the end of the tunnel" is actually progression through the wormhole. From what I can see, *this* universe appears to be one where everything is "as it should be". Our universe is... different... there is much pain and hurt everywhere, and at least half the time, nothing seems as it should be, and people have to work their whole lives just to find a sense of peace and contentment. But of course, that state ought to be our default, should it not? Why exist in any other state unless absolutely necessary, which, I am sure you will agree, by definition is unideal."

I nod. Strangely, I can follow him completely. He goes on.

"Therefore, those who have been here and returned, in the days before science, came up with the hypothesis of heaven."

"But what about hell?"

"Presumably another universe adjacent to our own. I'm not sure what determines within which a person will end up."

"But why do I perceive these hazy black shadows around the peripheries of my vision?" I say, surprised that I know the meaning and proper grammatical syntax to a word which I've never used before. Come to think of it, I notice my thoughts are clearer, more expansive, and significantly embellished. I have the impression that I've lived my whole life under a smothering, semi-translucent blanket of inferior intellect and lack of perspicacity, which has now just been cast off.

"You have that??" asks Bentley, as if he didn't expect it. I nod.

"That's the nonterminated philotic connection of the wormhole," Mickey explains. "It means that your link to the other dimension is still active – your body is still alive." He shrugs. "You're in a coma, back home."

I look at Bentley. "You were in a coma – does that mean you were here? Why did you go back?"

He makes a pained look. "Yeah... I was here... but I wanted to go back for you and Mickey, and even to tell Pa that Ma was here and she was okay, and he didn't have to be so angry and grieving anymore. I wanted you all to come back here with me. But when I got there, I found myself trapped in a body which didn't do what I wanted it to, and a mind which felt like cold molasses. I could barely function, and what is worse: I had unknowingly terminated the philotic connection of the wormhole – I couldn't go back until I died again, and in that reality, there was no way I could make that happen.

"So I just kept trying to get through to you and Mickey, and I finally found that I could communicate through Mick. It was a triumphant moment for me. I thought I'd at last be able to explain the truth, but then..."

"...But then I had that argument with Pa," Mickey cuts in, "And I decided that I was going to run away, rather than live there any longer with that maniac. I just wanted to get out of there."

I'm not listening. I've just had an idea.

"So... if I'm still alive... that means I can go back! I... I have to take care of something!" I can't contain my excitement.

But Bentley shakes his head. "Don't do it man, something could go wrong. It's not worth it, trust me – I was stuck in that body for *nine years*..."

I'm not listening; I'm concentrating on the blackness, the philotic connection to the wormhole – I'm willing myself back into my body. "I'll return soon, I promise!"

"No! Don't! Stop!" shouts Bentley, reaching out to me, but then the scene fades to white, like an overexposed picture, and the blackness crawls inwards from the outer reaches of my vision, chasing the white light back into a pinpoint, then snuffing it out altogether.

...

I gasp and sit up suddenly. I'm lying in a hostibul bed and tubes are jammed into my arms and I can hear a beeping noise which is hurting my head somethin' fierce, cuz I got a real big headache, like I bet Ma use'ta have. I sorta poke my head with my finger, and it smarts real good, but at least I know I'm alive, and I'm okay. For a moment, I can't quite sort it out – *did I just dream all that??* It seems pretty much like a muddy pond with a buncha little 'ol tadpoles swimming in it, and you can't see 'em properly, cuz they're too far down.

I remember seeing Bentley, and Mickey, and Ma, and I remember Mickey was talking about a buncha smart stuff that seemed to make sense to me at the time, but you know how it is with dreams: stuff seems proper that when you wake up it don't make no sense at all, but that's just how it is.

But still, I wonder, and the more I think about it, the more I am pretty dang certain it weren't no dream, and that there is something I gotta do... I think about it some more, and then I remember what it is!

I swing my feet over the side of the bed.

I'm thirsty.

...

"Gosh, it's like God copied the painter I seen in the art gallery in town!" Nina gasps, her breath almost a sigh. "I ain't never seen nothin' like this before, Fletch."

"What! Ain't you never before got up with the sun to go egg pickin'?"

"Well, shore I have but you know my house is all surrounded by trees so I don't get to see the sky way far away right down at the ground!"

"That's called the *horizon*," I say, feeling smart. Mickey taught me a buncha neat words.

"Ohhhh!" she says wondrously, squeezing my hand, and I feel even bigger.

The air smells like seaweed and fish and salt, and we're sitting down on the craggy bluffs overlooking the beach. An hour ago I snuck over to Nina's and collected her, and we came down in the dark. I wanted to show her the sunrise, 'cuz I knew it would be real pretty, and now we're here, and the sun

One Thread Short

is just yawning over the horizon, chasing the shadows away as it stretches out its long rays of deep reds and bright oranges and purples. It reflects in the water, too, and it looks like there's a golden, shimmering pathway going right up to the sun, like you could walk across it and in only a mile or two you'd be right up there in space, stepping onto that big ball of fire, easy as pie.

The sound of the ocean is like God breathing, only he's sleeping, so his breath is real soft and slow like it gets, just gentle rhythmic sighs, and I wonder if he's been sleeping ever since the 7th day, and that's why everything is all fucked up in the world, 'cuz he ain't been around to keep everything in line.

It's cold this morning, and the dewdrops are sparkling on everything, like millions of tiny diamonds. A faint breeze passes by, and I shiver, but it's only my back that's cold, 'cuz Nina's sittin' right between my legs, and so the front of me is warmer'n heck. I got my nose buried in the soft hair at the back of her neck and she smells like nothing I ever smelled before, and I can't describe it, but it gives me that real *BIG* feeling, like I used to get when I woke up in the morning and Ma had just made some fresh bread, and the sweet, warm smell of it fills my head, and for that one moment, it makes me feel like there's nothing wrong in any corner of the world.

That's how Nina smells.

My arms are around her waist, and she wriggles and hugs them and I swear she sorta purrs like a kitten, she's so happy, and I find myself wondering if maybe I ought not to do what I was gonna do. I get to thinking that when I'm with Nina I'm happier'n I ever been, and Ma used to say that you shouldn't break what ain't fixed. And even though everything's all busted up with Bentley and Mickey and Ma and Pa, well, Nina's *perfect*.

I lean over and reach inside my ratty ol' backpack beside me, and the thing I take out is heavy. I steal a glance at Nina and she's still enjoying the sunrise – I'm glad she can't see what I'm doing. It looks beautiful, though, and I almost wish she could see it. In the rich, warm light of the sunrise, the chromed steel seems like it's made of solid gold.

I think about Bentley, strong and handsome, and what it would be like to sit down with Ma and have a good long chat, and play ball with Mickey, and how nice it would be to think clear, and not feel so dumb all the time. Then I wonder about Nina again. Sure, everything is great *now*, but what about in ten years?

I just don't know...

"Look Fletch! Geese!" gasps Nina, pointing up into the sky like a child. Silhouetted against the fiery red sunrise is a V-formation of long-necked birds, honking away happily.

"That's beautiful," I agree, feeling the warmth of her body against mine, and the cold, heavy steel of the revolver in my hand.

[2016-08-06/12:09:12]

One Thread Short

Author's Note

Dear Reader,

I understand that some people may be offended by the derogatory language used in this story, specifically "retard" as used to describe people with disabilities. While I don't usually feel the need to explain myself, the truth is that I, too, have a disability, and endured many hurtful years of being called "retard", in school as a child. In this way, I am sensitive to the possibility that people may misunderstand my liberal use of the term as indicative that I have a lack of respect for these people. This is not my intention.

"Ethnocentrism" is the term used to describe the tendency of people to judge other cultures according to the moral standards of their own. This seems perfectly natural, but is often not reasonable. For example, we now believe slavery is wrong. 150 years ago, slavery was *not* wrong, according to the status quo of the era. This is because moral standards are inherently subjective, based on the time period and collective mentalities of the people within a culture. Indeed, one might argue that morality only exists in social situations – if we are all alone and our actions affect no living creature, nothing we do can possibly be considered wrong. A by-product of morality being tied to context and the subjective cultural climate is that moral standards change like seasons. Perhaps one day, slavery will be considered "right" again. Objectively, if the definition of morality is defined by a culture, and the moral majority of this society deems a phenomenon moral, therefore, the phenomenon is, by definition, not immoral, until the society once again undergoes a philosophical shift.

This is all philosophical semantics, but it is necessary to understand my intention behind this story. There are still many subcultures in North America which use the term "retarded" as a non-derogatory term for a person with a disability. In fact, it was only five years ago, in 2013, that the term "mental retardation" was removed from the Diagnostic and Statistical Manual of Mental Disorders, in the DSM-5.

It is easy to be judgmental of other cultures for not upholding our standards; it is more difficult to admit that, even in cultures which use languages and practices we don't approve of, the people within that culture are not all moral degenerates by default. It is perfectly possible for a person to be of high moral standard while doing something we consider morally defunct, if they are acting from a framework of subjective morality, with no maliciousness or ill will. My intent in freely using the term "retard" in a setting where it is entirely culturally acceptable, is to show that morality is not black and white, and that good, compassionate people exist as moral creatures by virtue of their intention, and should not be judged by taking their behaviour out of context and scrutinizing it from a sterile, alien perspective.

Respectfully,

~H.M. Friendly

Close your eyes.

You are looking at the sun. The sun is bright; it is hurting your eyes. Stop looking at it, don't look at it, you mustn't look at it. Look away and instead look down to your feet as they walk, and think about what you must do today. Step down cold grey steps to the concrete. Walk with certain secure footsteps. Today is a great day. There is another one who loves you. Yes, it is so; your fingers clench and unclench in a soft rhythm as you step. Follow behind yourself at a dog's level; only see your feet and calves in stiff black pants and glistening boots. Stop thinking strange thoughts; keep walking.

Enter a coffee shop nearby, look about very erratically. Look at the girl in the skirt in the corner and can you see her panties as she is crossing her legs? Don't do that; stop thinking these thoughts; Mother would be ashamed of you. Twitch and tap your feet; look at the old man sipping chai in the easy chair; wonder about his life and his wife and his car. Order some tea and follow yourself, again at dog's level and don't add any sugar or cream.

Go over to sit in the corner by yourself. Think about the great day ahead of you. You've had days like this before, many times before, but not for a long time now, and you are glad the moment has come. *Rejoice: there is another one who loves you.*

Look out through the window into the square. By the fountain a man and a woman sit. They are happy; they are laughing about something. See their white teeth. Nearby a small child, a boy, is running in circles on the cobblestones. His mittens hang from his jacket by strings. He is chasing pigeons. They flock on the ground in droves, and he runs within them, then giggles madly as the air around him explodes in a cacophony of wings, beaks and feathers. The man calls to the boy to come over; his shoe is untied so the man kneels down and fixes it.

Stop watching this scene. You are feeling very badly and you are having terrible memories of wonderful times when you were a boy, before you went to live with Gramma.

Stop thinking about this all. There is much to do today. Get up and leave this place.

Step quickly from the doorway and twitch. Walk with quick footsteps, ignore an echoing in your mind that someone is following you; walk to the highway and along it.

Sip your tea. Feel the wind and mud as cars surge past you. Sip your tea. Slow down, speed up; sip your tea. Don't think about the boy and the birds.

Close your eyes.

   Stop. View a dog in a hole. It does not live but grins widely. In a ditch its skin slides from its bloated body when you poke it with a stick. Poke its entrails. Push softly and impale and penetrate its gentle flesh with this stick and break it off inside. Throw the stick away.
   Start walking again. Sip your tea. It's not tea. Throw it away. Never look at it again. Turn around, stick out your thumb. Wish some pretty girl picks you up; it is raining on your body and your shirt sticks to your chest. No one stops.
   Never pay any attention to it; just keep walking; you're almost there. Look at the sky. It is dark and grey. Jump over a soggy ditch and quickly slip through bushes and bric-a-brac onto a hidden pathway very wet and clear to you. Follow yourself at rat's level and avoid the thorns who try and kiss and touch your legs. Step and step and step through mud and stones and your stomach hurts and growls. You wonder what it was you drank. It wasn't tea; you won't ever look at it again.

   STOP. Twitch and look and chew on yourself and dart around with your eyeballs because there is someone following you. Footsteps echo in your mind and you know they are following you. Listen very carefully for footsteps or breaking sticks but find you cannot hear them for torrents of screams and wails. *Suppress your thoughts.* No one is following you. It is all in your head, all from a known source – calm your heart and keep going.
   Follow yourself at shoulder level under low-hanging evergreen branches; use your strength to lift a boulder and see a hole below it. Prop the boulder up with a nearby stone. Enter the hole. The grass under the boulder is brown and slimy and wet. Put some in your mouth. Spit it out. Taste blood metallic on your tongue or wish to. Lower the boulder. Succumb to blackness.
   Lean your back against the wall of the hole, the muddy wall and slide down it to hunch at the bottom of the floor and sit in the dank soil. Sit with your hands between your legs and touch the worms slithering onto you and yourself. There is a great whistling in your head, a ringing in your ears, wind and a torrent of screams and wails. Your breathing is becoming very heavy and very maddening, and a terror is gripping you.
   Ok. Get up. *Get up.* Scramble with shaking hands; put fire to the torch you keep in a wooden box. Fumble with a flint. Spark it and see it white in your vision for many seconds after it is struck. It will turn red and then blue and will fade, but you've already lit the torch. Watch its fire. Watch it. Feel your terror receding. Follow yourself however low you wish, as you begin to move down a muddy tunnel. Notice how your shoes and your clothes have become unclean. Do not fret.

Close your eyes.

Things drip and fall into your hair but you are quite joyous. There is a smell wafting into your alert nostrils, and it is like dinner at Mother's and you wish to lick lips.

Emerge in a cavernous space. It is approximately eight meters wide by six meters long by two and a half meters tall. It is a cave of stone and earth, with rounded walls and ceilings. In some places, roots hang like tendrils from the ceiling, crawling through cracks in the rock. Your stomach jumps and growls and your heart is racing. You are sweating and you are beginning to get an erection. Put a hand down your pants. Take it out. Put it within the flame until it shakes and trembles and is very sorry and will not do it again. Put it away and keep going. Walk forward. Watch your step. Look around you.

There is a smell and it is like dinner to you. Kneel down now. Very artful and she is your creation, a changeling of your desire and revelations. She sits with her back against the wall. Do not poke her with a stick like a dog. She stares at you but only when you are above her and she loves you with white eyes and you know this. Lower your head to the ground. Gaze upon her face from eye level an inch away and marvel at how the flames play upon her softness. Touch the flesh of her cheek. Feel how it slides. Feel its warmth and the way it oozes when you push it. Push it again. See how it sheds a glistening nectar. Slide your tongue across her heavenly face. Put your tongue back in your mouth. She stares at you but only when you are above her and she loves you with white eyes and you know this.

Touch her with your careful fingertips in her soft area. Look at her face and her white lips and be sure she does not mind and is not offended. She does not, and she is not. Touch her and wait and smell her on yourself and wait.

Get up. Keep walking, slowly. View in the torchlight she and her and they and remember like you do of dinner at Mother's house, before the incident, when you ate the meat she placed upon your plate with sweet glaze for your tongue. They all love you. They all are lined up against the wall to watch. They like to watch.

No one followed you. You like this. Keep walking. Ignore the warmth in your pants and your persistent erection. *Do not touch it.* Keep walking, slowly.

Stop. Move your hand to that which you keep on your belt. It is a sheath of leather and now remove its child. She is a long blade that is curved and very shiny and has ivory and jade on the hilt. Look at it. Watch it. Feel its glow against your soft palm. Put it away now. Look up. Take a step forward.

Flames flicker red orbs in the back of her eyes. Walk closer. Ah, now you see. She loves you. She is a girl of the age eighteen or nineteen. Walk

Close your eyes.

to where she is bound on her throne of dirt and oak roots from far above, and sit on your own throne, where you belong, with her at your right hand. Smile because she trembles for you. *She loves you.* Get up and place the torch in its tall wrought iron holder close to her as she sits. Light the two other torches in their black iron sheaths on the wall to each side of the thrones. Stand very still and watch her. Watch how her thighs shake and she convulses with terror. She loves you but doesn't know it yet.

Walk to her and put your hand on her leg. The flesh of her body is bare and it shivers. Smile lovingly at her. Her hair is red; it is like brilliant flame in the firelight. The girl's eyes are wide, her sclera a brilliant white, her pupils, large black orbs. Her irises are a shining pale blue, and they are locked on yours. Her freckles look soft. Run your tongue over her face. Taste her. Watch her cringe and try to pull away.

Remove the dark cloth from her mouth. Listen as she says nothing but whimpers. See tears carve her face with reflective clarity of flame above. Speak to her softly and ask why she does not scream. Listen as she says nothing but whimpers.

Touch her with gentle fingertips in her soft area. Look at her face and her red lips and watch to see if she minds or is offended. She does, and she is. Your face is very close to hers and you can feel the heat emanating from her and she smells delicious. See the terror in her fleeing eyes and listen to her whimper louder than before and breathe sharply as you put your careful fingertips inside her warmth. Feel as she clenches and tightens. Kiss her because she wants you to inside. Penetrate her lips with your tongue and feel her pretty, gritted teeth. She makes noise now and tries again to pull her head away.

Grasp her soft throat with your hands and crush your fingertips into the middle of it just above her thyroids and behind her oesophagus. Listen to her breath labour, and delight in the feeling of her glands and organs so defined under your touch. Squeeze harder. Her hands struggle against her bonds, and she is saying stop, please stop, and she is crying. Take your hand from her throat and listen to her sob and try to ignore the murmuring erection in your pants. Watch her face contort and love it like that.

Speak to her when she asks you your motives not so eloquently as that, and comfort her like Gramma never did you when you ever were unhappy or bleeding and you would taste the wound like mother's meat dinners with glaze on them.

Go and sit down in an old wooden chair. Sit in the chair and the wood is broken in one place on the top left of the backrest and the upholstery is torn. Your stomach growls and hurts and you are hungry and you never had your tea and you don't know what it was but you won't ever look at it again. Lean back and sigh. Stretch your limbs. Crack your neck. Sigh. Feel

Close your eyes.

very terrible thoughts come into your head and run around in your head and throw things and screech and those people never could really get a hold of him or calm him down and how he kicks and bites and scratches and you feel these thoughts just like that. Begin to twitch again because these are bad thoughts and you do not like them. Shake your head about so you cannot think and your stomach growls and you are hungry. Put your head in your hands resting elbows on your knees and tear at your hair to not think. It is not working. You are losing yourself again into the blackness of your memories.

    Shake your head. Come back from inside yourself. Get off this chair. Stay focused. Today is a great day and you have a task. Get up and look at your prize. Stare at her and her very wet face. Ask her with a voice at which you are infuriated because it is very shaky and you don't know why, ask her if she is hungry because you know you are. Listen and watch her as she says nothing but whimpers.
    Become agitated with her lack of cooperation. Strike her in the face with your right fist and notice she's cut your middle finger with one of her teeth. Put it in your mouth like your Gramma never'd let you do and listen to her spit and choke and sob. Her nose is bleeding so go and taste and lick it and have her blood; fuck Gramma.
    Ask her patiently again if she is hungry and listen to her choke out the word No. You are unsatisfied; so hit her again; tell her she is being very rude and this time, after a moment's pause, she quietly sobs No Thank You. Feel very insulted that she is mocking you. Lose your patience and choke her with grated teeth. Put your fingers of the other hand inside her soft place and start with three and then four and force your way upwards very violently while explaining to her like Gramma did to you, that it is terribly rude to turn down someone's hospitality.
    You of course ask her again, like any good host would, and she coughs and chokes and sobs and screams at you, telling you this time that Yes, she is Fucking Hungry. As her shoulders convulse with her sobs, glistening saliva and blood intermingles to drip down her chin and onto her breasts and you suspect she is cold because of how her nipples present themselves to you.
    You are very very happy that she is hungry because you very much enjoy being a good host and you are also hungry so now it is dinnertime. Your stomach jumps in electrocution and you try to still your excited heart. Take your knife into your hand and cut the bonds of her right arm. Take her soft hand with your fingers. Try not to drool, and put her fingers in your mouth and feel them with your tongue and love it like she and all they

Close your eyes.

love you. Feel them tremble and listen to her strange noises of fear from her lips.

Remember fondly when Mother taught you to pare apples; take her long, slim index finger like that. Begin just below her middle knuckle and slice downwards against the bone like you are paring an apple. Stop for a second as she screams and jerks her hand away. Smile and close your eyes; listen to her cries of panic and pain and the strange things she is screaming at you and think of lovely music. Lick your lips as her flailing hand splatters blood all over them. Lean back and watch and enjoy as her hand is in front of her face and she stares incredulously at the strip of flesh hanging from her finger and bleeds all over her naked thighs and soft place. Cover your lips with your fingers and fail to stifle a mirthful giggle. She is being so funny! But it is dinnertime, and not the time for jokes.

Now take her hand again, and scold her for interrupting you and isn't she hungry? She doesn't answer but you don't care because you are excited and crossing your legs because of your erection that doesn't seem to want to go away and you wonder if that is healthy.

Hold her hand very still and continue to strip her fingers. Feel them jerk and tremble as you sever nerves and muscles and soon you giggle again because her fingers look like the gloves from the skeleton costume from the Halloween at Gramma's that one year. You frown and pause. Mother didn't get to see that Halloween costume. She never got to see any others and neither did Father. Not ever again and Gramma *hated* your skeleton costume.

Place the strips on a nearby round plate, in a straight line as you go, and when you are done sit back. Lick the blood from the gleaming steel. See that she appears to have passed out but you hadn't noticed because her screams are just like the ones in your head so you didn't notice when she stopped and they didn't.

Take her hand in yours and look at the meat still on the bones. Mother would have thought you could have done a better job. Take a torch from the wall and hold her skeletal fingers over the flame until the meat on them begins to crisp. See how she is not quite unconscious and she watches incoherently what you are doing but you know she can't feel the fire with her bones.

Gnaw the meat from her slender fingers.

Put the torch back on the wall. Light the four torches placed on a black wrought iron holder that has them at four corners, tilted in towards each other at the lit end, to form a small blaze.

There is a grill set above these torches that you got from an old barbeque; place the meat strips on them and watch them sizzle. Turn them frequently. They spit and crackle and jump in a certain oily way, like the

Close your eyes.

twisted, gnarled strips of bacon Father used to make. When they are most excellent, put them back on the plate. Taste one or two and they are very nice and sweet and you are satisfied and you beam like a child.

Sit again by her. Gently pat her cheek until she wakes up. Wait until she is mostly alert. She is no longer crying and you think she may have no tears left for now or has simply gotten numb.

Take her jaw in your left hand and open her mouth. Place two strips of meat onto her tongue and close her jaw. Tell her to eat her food. She chews twice, dazedly, and realizes that it is her own fingers. Frown as she spits them out onto the dirty floor and vomits upon herself. Feel very displeased. She's gotten vomit all over her soft parts, and wasted some lovely meat. She is being very ungrateful for your hospitality.

Carefully wash the vomit off of her with fresh water from a jug by the fire. Pick up the meat she has wasted. Shove it back into her mouth covered in dirt as her punishment for being so rude. Hold her jaw as she gags and wretches and writhes and tries to pull away and spit it out again. Her eyes are closed tightly in a most vulgar grimace, and little glistening diamond-like tears escape onto her cheeks as she futilely tries to avert her face from you. Summon up the courage to threaten that if she does not eat, you will cut off her tongue. (You feel badly about this because you don't like being harsh. She is your beautiful mistress and you love her and she loves you, even if she doesn't know it even yet.)

Smile benevolently, because you know she will soon learn, like all of they who came before her learned.

She eats. Watch her chew her meat and she has started crying again, silently blubbering now. Apologize for yelling at her and kiss her and stroke her hair.

Eat two more fingers. Ask her if she is still hungry. Watch as she stares helplessly at you for a few long seconds, with trembling lips and deeply anguished eyes, before she chokes out: Yes, she is. Is she very hungry? Yes, she is, she says.

You feel absolutely ecstatic at this opportunity to further be an excellent host, and that she is learning that she loves you like you love her. Divide the remaining strips in half. Give her the bigger pieces because she said she is very hungry. Feed her own finger-meat to her. Put the rest inside your mouth and chew. Taste it in your mouth and feel the warm glow of your seeping groin area. Feel your heart jump and become enflamed with love as you watch her there. Stroke her cheek and lick her right nipple with your tongue. Hear her gasp and whimper with terror. She does not yet understand, but it is okay: she soon will. Listen to her heartbeat and touch your crotch against her quivering leg to feel it tremble with your yummy bits. Hug her and touch her body with yours. Feel it

Close your eyes.

stiffen and tremble. Hear her breath quicken spasmodically, and her heart pound in her breast. Bury your nose in her neck with closed eyes and sigh blissfully and love her like Mother loved you when you were just a little one and very soft.

   Sit back. You are full of meat. You like it. Get up and extinguish the fire under the barbeque grill. You feel tired. Tell her it is time to sleep and you will sleep together tonight and she will love you. Bind her ankles and wrists together with coarse rope and release her from her throne. Carry her to the middle of the cavern and put her down in the red circle painted there. She will sleep there with you, and she will love you.

   Go and extinguish two of the torches. Move to extinguish the third but hear her voice from behind you in your mind. Follow yourself at chest level back to her and kneel over her delicious face. Open her jaw with your hand. Spit carefully and quietly onto her tongue and down her throat. Watch her gag and choke and cough and grimace. Ask her to repeat what she said. She needs to pee, she says. You realize you need to pee too.

   Thank her with great sincerity, and reveal yourself above her as she lies there. Urinate on her face and body and wash away all the dirty bad thoughts that Gramma put there. Watch her squirm and know it is because she is being purified.   Listen to her weep and sob and beat the floor with her skeletal hand and shriek in anguish and despaired rage. Know it is because she is being purified. She is learning to love you.

   Pick her up. Take yourself out of your pants and touch and rub her soft wet parts with it, for just a second. Feel yourself throb against her glistening damp warmth and heat. Feel guilty and look around because Gramma mustn't see that you just touched hers with yours. Put yourself away before you get too nasty before it is time.

   Cut her ankle bonds and walk her to the wall by your thrones where there is an old metal pail under the last lit torch. Stop and look around you and see with your mind all of them who like to watch and who love you like she does and will. Tell her she must pee in the bucket. Squat down in front of her so you can see she does ok, like you used to do with your puppy before you gave her a treat.

   You touched your puppy and then Gramma took her away, you remember... You don't know why. You frown, and don't think of it any longer.

   Watch her tremble and shake and try to pee. She manages a few pathetic dribbles and squirts but she seems shy for some reason. You realize she might not be able to pee when someone is watching, so touch her quickly and turn around because you respect her because you love her like all of them you can hear in your mind. After a little while, she urinates

Close your eyes.

and you can hear it on the shiny grey metal and feel it tickling the roof of your mouth and in your lower parts.

Turn around to lead her to your resting place. Feel surprise in your fingertips as you watch her lunge towards the wall with her bound wrists and grab the last lit torch with the hand that still has flesh upon it. Feel the skin on your face burning as she flings the torch at you and it hits you in your eye. Bend over momentarily and hold your eye and feel unhappy and that she must not love you and was misleading you. Become very angry that she betrayed you and straighten up with an infuriated roar. You cannot see anything because the torch has gone out and your eye hurts. Look for it with your hands. You cannot find it and you are worried about all them who like to watch and you love and who love you.

Become very silent. Listen. There is no sound. Walk softly. Listen. Feel her warm wetness in the air. Smell her. Listen.

Follow yourself at spider's level and prowl softly around your cave. *Stop. Listen.* You hear her breath against the wall to your left. Move in her direction, very softly. Hear her heart pound inside your temples. Feel the throbbing of your eye and your hidden area.

You are very close because you can smell her happy spot and the roof of your mouth itches because you want to taste it. Listen. Turn your head sharply to the left, against the wall. You can hear her breath in muffled gasps. She must be covering her mouth with her hand. You hear soft whimpering from deep in her throat. Move closer. Poise yourself to strike.

Fall to the floor as she shrieks and yells and dashes into your chest with her shoulder and stumbles and keeps running.

Get up and hear a wet sound. Hear scrabbling and slimy noises in the near distance. Slip on something and fall again and feel against the dirt to see what you stepped on. It is the torch. Fumble quickly for your flint from your pocket because you fear the noises and the smells you are sensing. Light the torch and blink and roar in pain as your eyes are seared with light and flame exploding in your face. Smell burnt hair and know it is your eyebrows and the hair from your nose. Stumble and allow your eyes to adjust once again. See the flame flickering against the walls. See all of them watching you and you know they are angry. Become very frightened. Rush towards the noises and the smells.

Illuminated in the flickering flame light, see her on all fours inside the wet slime, slipping and falling and trying to get up again. Feel electricity shoot all throughout your body and your head grow light and try not to faint. *She is **in** Gramma.* Watch in horror as her hands slip and slide through her entrails and organs and she falls and Gramma is all over her face.

Close your eyes.

Yell and feel dread flood over you and panic as Gramma turns her head and looks at you and her piercing, hollow eyes bore through your mind and you are in the cellar again. *Do not panic. Look at the flames.* You cannot look at the flames. Your eyes are petrified in Gramma's stare.

Snap out of it.

Turn away from Gramma's eyes to she who screams and wails and vomits and looks at you and cries with virginal fear. Rush to her and pick her up by the waist and throw her bodily across the room. She is covered in Gramma and now you are too, and it sticks to you and her voice is in your head again. Storm at a forward angle to her whom you have thrown and feel yourself in your brain convulsing and seizuring with rage.

Grab her slimy, matted hair with a shaking hand and drag her through the dirt across the floor back to your throne. Pull her to her feet by her hair and feel her scalp tug and stretch and moan. She is in front of you and screaming and it is in your ears and your body and you cannot stand it. Her face is contorted with anguish and is very sticky and dripping with a slow ooze and you hate it. *How can she do this if she loves you?* You feel a great and furious madness buzzing around the inside of your skull.

Strike her with your fist in her face with all your strength. Again. **Again.** Strike her and beat her and feel your knuckles fracture on her skull and her cartilage make a very wet crunchy sound.

Stop and breathe heavily. She is silent, finally. She hangs from her hair from your hand and her bent knees and skeletal fingers scrape against the floor. Saliva and blood oozes from her lips to the ground. Her nose twists at an odd angle and her jaw won't stay closed and wobbles back and forth. Check to see if she is still alive. She is.

Throw her by her hair to the floor at the foot of your throne. Watch with cold eyes and an aching fist as she hits the edge of her forsaken oak and falls forward to land on her face in the dirt between her legs.

You are very displeased with her. *She does not love you.* You do not love her. *She deceived you.* Pace up and down and twitch and convulse and seizure and think very bad thoughts that you can't stop this time. Scatter your eyes around the room.

Pick up the torch from the floor where you dropped it when Gramma looked into you. Put it back in its black iron sheath. Go to the corner of the cave and pick up a large jar of fuel and bring it back to where you were standing before. Refuel the two torches on either side of the thrones, and the one in its tall narrow iron holder. Light this one, and keep the others dark. Place the fuel on the ground near it.

Calm down. Breathe. Stay away from Gramma. Do not look that way. Wash your hands. Don't touch yourself. Look at her on the floor with her

Close your eyes.

head between her spread legs and her face in the dirt. Go over to her. Use the container of water to carefully wash Gramma off of her skin. Make sure she is clean all over.

Pick her up and carry her to the red circle where you will sleep. Place her down. Look at her. Look at her soft parts. Feel the pulsing within yourself and your trousers and know it is now time. Climb astride her. Pour cold water down her throat to moisten her and wake her up as she chokes and splutters and coughs. Take her head in your hands and look lovingly into her wild eyes. Stroke her clean wet hair. You will forgive her. She will love you, and it will purify her.

Tell her that it is time and she will love you whether she wants to or not. Do not feel bad this time when you threaten her and carve the flesh of her breast in patterns you see in dreams or nightmares. Feel her lack of strength to resist. Feel her apathy. View her deep wounds and the bright red blood that pools in them. See very large white fat cells. Gouge two or three out and put them in your mouth and eat them with your teeth and your tongue.

Spread her legs and feel wet heat and smell sweet tanginess and tongue the roof of your mouth as it itches. Stare at her soft fiery hair and the triangle it forms and play with it with your fingers in little circles. Remove your clothes and uncover yourself to the dark heat and look at the way you throb and pulse. Bend and become her and lose yourself in a cavern of red stars and drippings. Watch her breasts move and her sticky blood smear into the sweat of your flesh. Put your ear to her mouth as you prod and lunge. Listen to her breath and the soft cries which echo from deep within her throat. Feel her limp body under you and watch her eyes stare at nothing at all. Touch her mind and feel her withdrawing and falling into a depthless chasm of her own internalizations. *She is learning to love you.*

Experience yourself as a child and all your bad thoughts explode and close your eyes as there is a tremendous pain in your brain and an overwhelming of your lower parts as all they whom you love watch you and love you.

Feel a great exhaustion of a slippery sticky void grasp your body. Lay beside her and hurtle into yourself and dark cellars with rough wooden doors and creeping cobwebs under the stairs.

Open your eyes.

Notice she is not beside you any longer.

Close your eyes.

See that your carving knife is no longer in its sheath. Feel confused and bewildered. Sit up suddenly and turn around. You can see her now. She is moving slowly and painfully across the floor. Narrow your eyes. Zoom your vision to its focal point of your knife grasped in her left hand. She must have cut herself free. She is turned away from you. Lay still and observe her for a moment. Watch as she drags herself through the dirt by her left forearm and right elbow, her right hand hanging, useless, from the wrist. She is barely crawling, slithering through the dirt like a worm, her wretched, naked body filthy with blood and grime. Labouriously, she rises to her knees, her face a perfect picture of tragedy and strife. She attempts to stand, but unwittingly tries to support her weight with her fleshless right hand. She gasps sharply and cries out as she falls back to the dirt, quickly suppressing her vocalizations with the crook of her arm. She lies, writhing in the dirt, like an animal, making small, pathetic noises from deep within her chest, anguished moans she tries hard to crush into nothingness. Her forehead shines with glistening beads of sweat. Her body is smeared black and gritty with coagulated blood and dirt. Her breath is rapid and heavy and ragged and she is swallowing repeatedly, a thick, guttural noise interspersed with gasps and moans. Abruptly, her spine arches and she vomits violently into the dirt. Recognizing that it is composed of bile and her own fingers, she recoils physically from it, and gags again, but it is a dry heave which terminates in a hacking cough.

Presently, she drags herself over to her undeserved throne. With sublime effort, and impressive imprecations, she pulls herself to her feet under support of her left hand. She stands still for a moment, weaving unsteadily. She is silhouetted in the flickering orange flame light. The curve of her spine resembles a dying tree, drooping earthwards, but not yet fallen.

She straightens up, and, taking hold of the torch in the wrought iron holder, she begins to make her way to the opening from which she saw you emerge when you first arrived. You feel a sense of panic and betrayal. *She is leaving you!* Prepare to arise and give chase!

Abruptly, she stops, and looks back. You remain still. You watch; curiosity, then relief replaces your panic, as she turns and staggers slowly back to the thrones. *She has learned to love you!* She cannot bear to leave you. Yes, you know it is so! Your heart swells with joy.

Your relief reverts to curiosity as you continue to observe her actions. She has returned the torch to its holder, placed the knife down on the throne, and has bent to awkwardly pick up the glass jar of fuel using her left hand and right wrist.

Watch her as she pours fuel from the large jar all over your beautiful oaken thrones. She curses and grits her teeth as the caustic gasoline splashes onto her and invades her deep wounds.

Close your eyes.

For a moment, you are dumbfounded. You almost cannot believe your eyes. You come to the conclusion that she wishes to burn you and your thrones and all those who love you. Feel within your brain a paroxysm of a roaring, flaming rage. She has betrayed you, and forsaken your hospitality! Feel like Gramma for a very small second.

Rise to your feet. You plan to charge at her and make her feel like Gramma made you feel when you didn't eat all of your liver that one day but never again after that. You are unable to suppress a choking growl of rage.

She turns around. She must have heard you. Fear and surprise attach themselves to her face and then, with a great effort, she propels the jar of fuel at you. Feel the glass explode against your face and embed itself into your flesh. Roar at the burning of your eyes and the choking of your lungs as you are saturated with fuel.

You are very unhappy that she keeps hurling things at your face.

Open your eyes finally to see her rushing at you with your knife. Your white eyes are surprised as she sinks the blade very deep into your breast with an animalistic snarl most unbecoming of a lady.

Shoot your hand out quickly and grab a hold of her right arm as she tries to run. Hold her and feel pain in your body and it is slightly hard to concentrate because something is wrong. She reaches out with her left hand and grabs the lit torch in its narrow iron holder and crushes the embers directly into your face.

Hear a noise and sense a tingling sensation as your body envelops in flames. You smell something sharp and acrid. Pay it no mind.

Pull the knife from your breast and hear it gurgle with your left ear. You find breathing difficult, and you are choking on something thick and wet and metallic.

With all your strength, carve into her throat with its blessed edge. Her head falls back obscenely. You can see her spinal cord, and the white **O** of her oesophagus.

You smell something bitter as your body roasts and crackles. You are dizzy and you are about to fall over. There is a great pain overwhelming your senses.

Look into the girl's eyes to see a strange and cloudy presence. Close your eyes and feel her blood gush in ebbing pulses and flow down your body with your own and now there is no more wailing in your head, and for a moment, you feel surprised, and glad.

You are having difficulty concentrating.

Fall down very deep into the black cavern of your memories.

Close your eyes.

Crawl back from inside yourself; *you are slipping and falling down a steep cliff;* crawl back from inside yourself...

You cannot breathe. You cannot feel your skin. Flame is embracing you all over. Look at the girl. Her eyes are dark. Her red mane has been transformed into an angelic crown; it is alive and hungry!

Now you see that she *does* love you! She did this for you! The two of you!

Stumble with her to your godly thrones and place her in her rightful position. Lose your balance and fall into your own seat. Hear a noise like dragon's breath as the oak ignites in blissful fury. See flames lick your eyes and flicker like birthday parties and beautiful joy, all over the walls of your cavern. Watch all of them who are lined up against the walls watching you. They smile stiff and happy.

She and they all love you.

[2006-03-10 21:45:38]

Made in the USA
Columbia, SC
31 July 2017